THE TRANSFORMATION

THE TRANSFORMATION
Robin Buckallew

Saffron Books
2018

First Printing: 2012

ISBN 978-1-105-93003-4

Saffron Books

Cover design by: Mat Jones

To Dr. Gloria Caddell, because all scientists stand on the shoulders of other scientists.

Typha breathed a sigh of relief as the TV face ended the daily news and signed off for the night. She looked around her small room, only ten feet square, but hers, and reflected for the thousandth time how lucky she was to have so much space all to herself while her neighbors on every side shared their small spaces with large families. She wished only that she could gain more control over her private space.

The news man dominated the space when he spoke and she longed to turn off the set. Unfortunately, television was controlled from Central Control and she watched television when the elders wanted her to watch television, which was most of the time. The elders encouraged watching television because it reduced the crime rate and prevented deviant behavior…at least, that's what the council claimed. She hadn't seen any evidence for their assertion, but most people accepted it since they were brought up in a society which repeated it endlessly. "Turn on the TV, keep your town crime free"…repeated again and again in the schools, in the churches, in the shopping centers.

TV was everywhere…in the schools, in the churches, in the shopping centers. If you went for a walk, which was discouraged, there were televisions in every window, at every street corner, and even embedded in sidewalks. The television in her room took up the entire wall, so when it was on it was impossible to avoid. Changing the channel brought little relief; in spite of hundreds of channels, there was a dreary sameness to all the stations.

You could watch news, inspiration, game shows, or a seemingly endless array of dramas or comedies in which high minded families struggled against hordes of evil people trying to tempt them off the proper, accepted pathway into non-conformity. The ending was predictable; the forces of good won against the forces of evil and conformity triumphed. It was hard to discern any possible plot you hadn't seen so many times you could practically mouth the words by heart. Small cosmetic differences didn't vary the plot enough to make the story interesting.

Typha stretched and contemplated going out for a forbidden evening walk. It was past 8:30 and everyone was expected to be home, ready to go to bed after an evening of enjoying TV with their family. With no family, Typha was a little freer to pursue her own interests in the evening.

She sighed again, this time in regret…all her interests were illegal. She longed for her books, forbidden books, stashed safely in the hiding place where her grandfather stored them decades ago, keeping a promise to his mother that her books would never be relinquished to the endless fires which lit up the night in his generation. Typha never experienced the fires; they ended years ago as the disgraced books turned into ashes. Now the elders conducted burnings in secret when the police confiscated stashes of horded books.

Tonight, Typha decided, was not the night to read. The news was full of the latest panic, a new uprising of the resistance, and the streets were more heavily guarded than usual. Tonight was not the night for a walk in the darkened streets.

Typha groaned, sick of her cowardice in the face of overwhelming need. Her great-grandmother would never act so afraid. Her great-grandmother would march right out there, taking a defiant stroll through the guarded streets, daring them to shoot her.

Rolling over on her hard mattress, she punched her old, thin pillow a few times in a hopeless attempt to fluff it up. Lights out…right on the dot of 8:45. A crackdown was always accompanied by an early curfew. The elders were prompt, she had to give them that. Typha lay on her back in the dark room, hands behind her head, and tried not to think. Sleep at this hour was hopeless enough. It would be even more impossible if she allowed herself to think.

Anna turned, her senses tingling with a sensation of eyes burning through her skin. She smiled, a smile containing a world of meaning, a smile of welcome, a smile of love and joy. Simon held out his arms and she practically flew into them.

"Welcome home", she purred. "I've missed you."

The embrace was long and deep, and Anna nestled against Simon's chest. Man, he smelled good! He smelled of old leather and parchment, just like an old library where one can search for ancient treasures in print. Anna loved books and nothing made her happier than being married to an antique book dealer. She considered herself the luckiest woman in the world, because he was also kind and gentle, tender, and loved her as thoroughly as she loved him.

"I'm just about to wrap up here", she said, flipping off the light on the microscope and reaching for the plastic cover. "I'll join you on the walk home. Is it still raining?"

She reached for the umbrella she kept at work for emergencies.

"No, it's a beautiful evening", Simon answered. "If we hurry, we can still see the last traces of the sunset".

Anna sighed with contentment. This was going to be a wonderful evening. Walking home with Simon in the sunset was the most glorious way she could imagine to end her day. She spent most of the day at the prairie, gathering data for her latest biodiversity study, and only came in when it started to rain. It wasn't that she wanted to come in; after all, she worked in the rain many times. The plants didn't mind the rain, or run from it. They thrived on it, and so did she. But she was working with a group of students today and she realized some time ago that students became petulant and whiny when asked to work in the rain. She yielded to the majority and allowed the group to complete the afternoon in the comfortable, dry, climate-controlled lab.

Since 2:00, she was hunched over her dissecting microscope, working on identification of the specimens they collected in the morning. There were over a hundred new specimens to identify and preserve. She also had at least a thousand photographs to download and sort. Although Anna herself was a botanist, primarily interested in the plant community, the group collected a number of insects, and these also needed to be sorted and catalogued. Anna spent much of her afternoon preserving the tiny specimens. Her eyes were tired and she was eager to be outside again, walking hand in hand with Simon under the sunset. She locked the lab with a spring in her step, all the fatigue of a few minutes ago forgotten.

The walk home was a short one, only a quarter mile, but it always seemed so rich, especially at this time of the evening. Dark trees stretched stout branches toward the sky, rustling in the gentle breeze which stirred their leaves. Fireflies flitted, their small lights glimmering softly in the near dark. The air was fresh with the smell of the recent rain, a smell that always made Anna feel like a child again, running through the wet grass with her friends, seeing who could get the wettest in a game of stomp the puddle. The lights of the university were also familiar, comforting like an old friend who knows you just enough to like you, but not enough to feel contempt.

Yes, it was a good feeling tonight. Anna was happy, so happy she was almost skipping. Simon squeezed her hand, letting her know he was happy, too. Words weren't needed for communication; they'd been together a long time and they knew each other well.

Anna and Simon owned a small, homey house near the university. Though not as large as the homes of many of the other professors, it was roomy enough to hold them and all their books, and still have room for two cats. Plus, it was paid for and they had few worries about the future.

Their only son was grown, and graduated last year from a theatre program on the west coast. He was working this summer in a Shakespearean company in San Francisco and they were very proud. They splurged some of Anna's summer teaching pay on a ticket to San Francisco to see him play Iago. It was a wonderful trip and they were still basking in the glow of it, weeks later.

The even tenor of their life was almost enough to keep them feeling insulated from all the radical changes taking place around them, in the political and social milieu…almost, but not quite. Anna wore a worried frown as they unlocked the door of their little castle, but for once Simon didn't notice. He was eager to share a gift he bought for her during his trip to Belgium.

"Guess what I got for you?" Simon's eyes gleamed with anticipation, holding his hands behind his back, teasing her, making her guess.

"A Belgian waffle?"

Simon shook his head at her deliberately silly guess.

"A German sausage?"

Again Anna guessed deliberately silly. She and Simon played this game often and even when they knew the answer, they would miss. After all, missing was what made the game fun.

"Hercule Poirot?"

Once again, a shake of the head, a big grin, and Simon produced the package from behind his back. It was neatly wrapped, with the characteristic sharp corners she expected on presents from Simon. He was always careful and it showed in his gift-wrapping, as in everything else he did. The package, not unexpectedly, was square and solid.

"Oh, a book! What a wonderful surprise!"

Anna played the game. Of course it was a book; she and Simon both loved books, lived for books, and Simon was a rare book dealer. He had access to books other people hadn't even thought of purchasing yet.

Her eyes gleamed as she ripped open the paper with considerably less neatness than Simon put into wrapping it. Anna was neat herself but when it came to presents, she was still a small child. Presents brought a glow to her face that made her look considerably younger than her 50 years, which was one reason why Simon, who adored her, made sure to never come home without one.

"Oh, Simon, it's perfect! A first edition Darwin!"

She threw one arm around his neck as she carefully turned the yellowed pages with her other arm.

"Oh, my God! It's autographed!"

Anna fell on the couch in stunned silence. A first edition *Origin of Species*, complete with the autograph of Charles Darwin himself. This was too much. This must have set Simon back a year's salary!

"How?"

"Oh, I have connections", Simon said breezily.

He didn't plan to share with her the adventures he went through to get this particular book for her; it was better she didn't know how much he paid for it. The credit card would groan for a while…quite a while…but it was worth it to see the pleasure on her face. She'd been too grim lately, too worried, with all the odd rumblings coming out of Washington, out of the university, and out of Colorado Springs. More than anything he lived to see her smile, and she was certainly smiling now. Tomorrow would be time enough to face the worries again. He wanted to enjoy this homecoming tonight.

He insisted she sit in the living room and rest while he disappeared into the small kitchen to prepare a special supper. He never suffered from jet lag and came home from an overseas trip bursting with energy. She was tired and he was going to spoil her. She deserved to be spoiled now and then, as hard as she worked, and as committed as she was to protecting what remained of the environment. He wouldn't tell her tonight about the rumors he heard in the airport on his layover.

Dinner was a festive occasion. Chicken with sautéed onions, fresh vegetables, and a home made strawberry cheesecake. Simon was a good cook, every bit as good a cook as Anna herself, and both of them enjoyed cooking for each other.

After the dishes were done, they lay together on the sofa and debated whether to turn on the TV or just read together for the rest of the evening. Simon, remembering the rumors in the airport, voted for reading. Anna agreed without hesitation. She wasn't interested in television and only watched it occasionally, mostly to humor him. She was an avid reader and preferred to spend the evening with a good book, anyway.

The beautiful late summer evening beckoned, and they spent the rest of the evening reading on the porch, watching fireflies and listening to the crickets. Occasionally they heard the unmistakable croak of a bullfrog from the little pond on campus.

The evening was beautiful, peaceful, and just what Simon could hope for in a homecoming. Although he did get a little reading done, he spent most of the evening watching his beloved Anna, her hair shining in the moonlight, still natural brown in spite of her age, with only a few strands of gray giving away the fact she wasn't the same college freshman he'd fallen in love with. Her face was smooth and youthful, with a hint of lines beginning to show around her eyes. She rarely wore make-up but he liked her with the natural look, her blue eyes sparkling as she curled up beside him with her book. He didn't even notice the slight middle-age bulges which gave her once slim figure a matronly look. After all these years of marriage, he still marveled that this special woman would have chosen him out of all the men she knew.

He sighed contentedly. Everyone should be so happy.

6

Typha turned the corner cautiously. In recent weeks, she felt like she was being followed and this was a dangerous enough corner without the thought that someone could be lying in wait for her. Nothing happened and she relaxed.

The buildings pressed close together on each side, their walls rising 120 stories and abruptly ending as they reached the dome. These buildings grew as tall as they could. The dome prevented any building being more than 120 stories tall.

Typha glared up at the dome. She wished she could see outside, see the sunlight, see the real world as it once existed. She wished she could see a tree, a flower, or an animal, any animal. She knew her thoughts were subversive but she didn't care. After all, she was already on every possible list she could be on, so what did it matter? They expected her to think subversive thoughts. They knew she was thinking subversive thoughts. It was in her DNA, right? At least, that's what her file said.

First there was her great-grandmother, fighting against the great transformation from the start, resisting to the end, refusing to turn over her books, refusing to turn over the keys to her lab, standing in the way of the bulldozers as they tried to plow up her beloved prairie. Then her grandfather, using his connections in theatre to produce performance pieces challenging the new way, criticizing the changes in the government, refusing to shut the theatre doors when he was closed down, always finding new performance spaces when they shuttered or burned one theatre after another.

Her mother, her beloved mother, followed the path blazed by her father. Her mother, like her great-grandmother, chose to study science. Though all the schools were closed to her and she wasn't allowed any formal training in the sciences, she used her grandmother's books and equipment to teach herself, down in the secret hideaway which housed all the forbidden books…not just her great-grandmother's books, but all the books saved by members of the resistance, protected from the fires which consumed so many pages without mercy.

Typha was born underground, in the hideaway, and raised in the company of the resistance. She was born subversive, she was raised subversive, and now, though much less openly, she lived subversive, a loyal member of the resistance, in spite of working every day for the very government they were in resistance against.

Yes, Typha was expected to be thinking subversive thoughts and she indulged herself. A tree...she tried to conjure up a tree in her mind, but since there were no more trees on Earth during her lifetime, she had never seen a real one. She did have her grandmother's books, and all the specimens of plants and insects the older woman collected in her life.

Her mother passed on all the science to Typha and now she was in a position to use her knowledge. Although women as a rule weren't allowed to work, Typha was an undesirable, unable to get permission to marry because of her unacceptable lineage. Besides, the elders needed someone who understood Botany and interest in the topic withered after the plants went extinct. The elders needed someone to cultivate the tissue cultures so vital to the preservation of life.

The cultures were the only thing standing between the human race and total annihilation, since they were the only possible means of producing the oxygen everyone needed to breathe. So Typha was brought on board to keep the cultures alive in an inhospitable environment. She held the future of the entire species in her hands.

With all this going through her head as she passed through the narrow alleys, she glanced absently down at her hands as if expecting to see them growing grotesquely large. They were, as usual, small and neatly kept, nothing grotesque, and undeniably feminine.

Typha, in spite of her status as an undesirable, was very pretty and male heads turned her way as she walked. She was also, to be totally fair, the only woman on the street at this hour except for the shapeless, faceless mob of homeless who were an eternal presence. The housewives waited until the streets were clear of men going to work before they ventured out to complete their daily routine. This was mostly from habit, since with all the homeless, the streets were never completely free of men.

The church bells rang as Typha entered the giant building which housed the only scientific lab left in the country. In spite of herself, Typha cringed visibly. Church bells at this hour could only mean one thing: they'd caught a member of the resistance and were taking them to the Interrogators for questioning.

Few people were able to survive questioning long enough to have an actual trial; those few that did were given mock show trials and put to death in the public square. She made a mental note to try to contact the resistance through the network and see if she could get any information. Who was captured? The question plagued her all day, the macabre visions providing a grim accompaniment to her almost automated efficiency.

Her mother's death at the hands of the interrogators forced Typha to take the interrogations seriously. She still remembered how she felt as she stood helplessly, looking on as her mother was "questioned" to death. Only sixteen at the time, Typha knew the interrogators would start on her next; after all, what they seemed to want to know was the identity of her father. Scared and cold, hungry from being held without food in a dark cell for 72 hours, the teenager choked back terror as she watched her mother defy her tormenters and refuse to scream, cry, or beg. Without a word, Mom turned her head to one side and died, strong and proud, and still just as pretty as when she'd been alive, in spite of the bruises.

Typha died a bit herself that day. Her whole life centered around her mother. All her education, all her social network, everything centered on this one woman, now smaller and paler than she was in life, her body stiffening from rigor mortis, her unquenchable energy drained by the brutal enemy she spent her life fighting.

As the interrogators turned in her direction, she let out a small squeal, in spite of all her efforts to be as brave as her mother. Cupping a hand over her traitorous mouth, she straightened her spine and faced the interrogators defiantly. To her surprise, they simply passed by, leaving her to collapse in a heap on the floor and await her fate.

Her fate wasn't long in coming. An elderly man helped her to her feet and swept her out the door before she could take time to look back, almost as though he was afraid she'd turn into a pillar of salt. She was brought before the elders and her fate decided with one swift stroke…she was going to be the official government botanist. After all, they just killed the only remaining scientist (at least, that they knew of) who could help them out of their terrible plight.

That was ten years ago. Typha worked quietly for the government for ten years, working even more quietly for the resistance at the same time. She never forgot her mother's death and now, as the church bells accompanied her to her lab, she sank into a despondent mood readily noticeable to Joshua, her partner and apprentice.

"So, what's wrong?" Joshua snarled.

Joshua wasn't happy to be working with, and trained by, a woman. He thought it was a violation of the natural order of things, and he didn't hesitate to be as difficult as he could most of the time. He also thought there was something suspicious about such an attractive woman who hadn't gotten married and had several kids by now.

"Nothing, really", Typha answered evasively.

She didn't want to get into a pissing contest with Joshua, and she had no intention of revealing her background to him. She and the elders were in agreement on the advisability of keeping her history a secret from everyone else.

Pulling on her lab coat, she stepped over to check the cultures Joshua prepared. As usual, he'd gotten them all wrong and they spent the rest of the morning trying to straighten out the mess he made. They worked in silence, her disapproval of his lackluster performance hanging heavy in the air between them. He sullenly followed along as she explained, for perhaps the hundredth time, just exactly how the cultures needed to be set up if they were going to survive.

"What's it really matter, anyhow?" Joshua pouted as they settled in for lunch. "A bunch of stupid cells on a petri dish, and you act like somehow the world depends on getting it right."

Typha turned on him, so sick of his whining she couldn't hold it in any more.

"The world *does* depend on our getting it right!" she yelled, out of control for perhaps the first time in her life.

Typha prided herself on her ability to control her emotions, but exhaustion, anger, and fear were starting to get the best of her.

"The world relies on these cultures for the very air we breathe, and if they die, we die. Get it, Joshua? This *is* life as we know it, and our very existence depends on these cells you treat so casually and carelessly. These are life, and don't you ever forget it!"

She became aware she was shouting and her tone was much less pleasant than the detached, patient tone she usually used in a professional setting. This wasn't her first apprentice; so far, there hadn't been any man willing to complete the training because they felt it was demeaning to work for a woman. She tried to maintain her patience, but now she was beyond patience. She heard the door to the

10

inner chamber slide open; in a moment, one of the elders stood in the lab, a place they almost never ventured to enter.

"What's going on here?"

Although there was no obvious disapproval in his voice, the undertones were so sinister both Typha and Joshua shivered. Neither of them wanted to get the elders mad. The elders held everyone's future in their hands, and they weren't afraid to sacrifice a small and unimportant life for the cause they believed in devoutly.

"What exactly is the meaning of the shouting?"

He looked at Typha as he said it; it was obvious he knew she was the one who raised her voice and disturbed his tranquility.

"Nothing I can't handle, sir", Typha said quietly, her head obediently bowed.

She glanced out of the corner of her eye at Joshua; he, too, stood with his head bowed in respect and admiration. Joshua was a believer in the cause; he was truly an insider, in a way she, as a female and a subversive, never could be.

"We were just having a discussion about the proper way to plate the cultures, and I'm afraid I got carried away. I raised my voice without thinking. It won't happen again, I promise".

Typha knelt in front of the elder to demonstrate the sincerity of her apology, all the while fuming at the need for such groveling subservience to a man who had no knowledge of how the world worked outside his own study. The elder hesitated, then looked at Joshua.

"She was totally unreasonable, sir", Joshua sputtered. "She was talking to me like I'm some sort of woman, sir, just another housewife."

He was angry, humiliated, and his words tumbled one over the other in his eagerness to get her in trouble and end this unsatisfactory situation. He was clearly aiming to get himself reassigned to a male boss.

"She thinks she has some sort of jurisdiction here, and she makes me do the most demeaning things, like water all these stupid, irrelevant plant cells. I'm just wasting my time here, spinning my wheels in women's work, and then she flies off the handle, yelling at me like I have to listen to her or something..." Joshua trailed off, puzzled by the look on the elder's face.

Could it be he just committed a serious blunder? After all, this *was* women's work, so why was the elder looking at him like that? This couldn't be important, or they wouldn't have a woman in charge of it. Typha recognized the wheels turning in his head and filled in the familiar litany of male complaints from memory.

The elder frowned, showing uncharacteristic signs of tiredness and disappointment.

"Joshua, we selected you for this position because we have faith that you have the calling, that you truly believe in the cause. We really do need someone mature and responsible in this position. I'm sorry we have to subject you to the supervision of a woman, but rest assured, it's only temporary, until you're fully trained and able to take over the management of the lab yourself. If this wasn't important, we wouldn't have put you here. We feel it's too important to leave in the hands of a woman, but right now, we don't have any choice. I have great things planned for you, son, and I need you to listen carefully and learn. It's the only hope for the continued survival of our civilization."

He turned on his heel and left without saying anything to Typha, still on her knees on the floor, stunned. Joshua...an elder's son? Joshua destined to be an elder? And they put him in here with her? Terror crept over her. Yes, indeed, she was being watched.

4

Anna frowned over the morning paper. The president was going to speak to the country tonight and everyone was urged to tune in and listen. The message was very important, according to the AP.

Anna remembered when this president took office two years ago. The country was in a tough spot and overwhelmingly voted to elect a long shot, someone who two months before wasn't given much chance of winning. The new president was one of the most personable they'd elected in a long time and he managed to exude hope in every speech. In addition, he didn't have any of the vices so common in recent decades. He was committed to a very happy marriage, he was emotionally stable and mature, he was open to new ideas, and he was ready to end an unpopular war.

The war hadn't ended; in fact, it was growing larger every day. Instead of being at war with one country, they were now at war with all of Asia, and Egypt just declared war on them, as well. The hard line religious rhetoric of the previous president was replaced with a softer, gentler rhetoric. Lots of Jesus talk and soft words about the Prince of Peace replaced the constant God on Our Side posturing, but the faithful Muslims were not mollified. It was still Jesus vs. Mohammed as far as they could tell, and the Christian soldiers carried bigger guns. So they continued to join the insurgency in larger and larger numbers, and one by one, countries signed on for what was becoming a new world war and a new Crusades all rolled into one.

As an atheist, Anna had little use for the constant religious taunting thrown around on both sides and she felt there was a lot of reason to be worried if either side won. Now the president was addressing the nation to give them encouragement, hope…to rally the troops around a united front, he said at the last pep talk, only two weeks ago.

These "neighborly" chats of the president were getting more frequent as various factions in the country stirred up their own followers, some in support of the president and some in rebellion. Both sides declared their determination to fight for God's country and God's law, both of them shouting from the same Bible, though with no ability to agree on exactly what it was God wanted them to accomplish. The academics huddled in their offices, continuing the work of education and research as though nothing was happening in the world outside their walls. They were aware of the disturbances and the unrest but preferred not to take sides.

Anna leaned back in her chair. Her head throbbed. She closed her eyes and massaged her temples, hoping to get some relief before she headed back to the lab for another long day. She thought about the last two years, the escalating hostilities, the growing divisions in the country, and her head throbbed so hard she thought it would burst apart if she moved.

At first the new president exuded calmness and politeness, urging everyone to work together. Most people assumed he'd end the constant interference of religion in the government. Though an openly religious man, he believed in the Constitution, and besides, his God was a nice, gentle God...Jesus the Prince of Peace. Even as he made moves to increase the role of God in government, most of his followers weren't worried, even many of those who fought against the intrusions of religion in government affairs under the last president. Even if he does bring in a little bit of government sponsored prayer now and then, he's tolerant, his God is tolerant, and so everything will be all Age of Aquarius, and we'll all be welcome and happy under his administration.

Anna worried, though. She didn't like the look of it. She'd studied enough history to be aware of how many times tolerance disappeared with the acquisition of power. She didn't trust anyone who wore religion on their sleeve. Even as a child, when she still believed in Santa Claus, the Easter Bunny, and God, she felt uncomfortable with those who went around publicly announcing their piety to anyone who would listen. It just didn't feel right.

Anna worried when the religious rhetoric accelerated, slowly at first, then more and more. She worried they might be like the proverbial frog, slowly having the heat raised until at last they found themselves boiled to death.

In addition, Anna worried about the increasing threats to the environment. She'd worked as an ecologist for a long time and she was seeing changes which were worrying her. Yesterday, out in her prairie, she found surveying stakes. This wasn't supposed to happen. This was a protected area, off limits to developers.

She asked her department chair if he knew anything about it, but he was unaware of anything changing in the ownership status or the protected status of the prairie. He said it was probably just something the Corps of Engineers put there to mark a survey they were doing. Anna didn't believe it; this wasn't a Corps property, and he should have been aware of that. This property belonged to the school. Anna was in charge of all research in the area and no one approached her about doing a survey. Besides, the stakes didn't look like an ecologist's markers; they looked like a developer's markers.

Simon shuffled into the dining room, yawning, looking like a tousled little boy in his plaid pajamas. Well, okay, like a gray-haired tousled little boy with the beginnings of a middle aged spread, but still youthful and energetic.

He rummaged for a glass, poured milk and made some toast. He settled into the chair at the other end of the dining table and reached to the floor for the paper Anna discarded. Anna kept her eyes closed, massaging her temple, thankful the aspirin was beginning to take effect.

Simon lost himself in the paper, starting as always with the sports section. He'd get to the local and world news soon enough; first, he needed to know how the Cubs were doing. Simon loathed the Cubs, and it always gave him a good start to his day to read the news if they were doing poorly. This morning, as Anna already knew, there was a pleasant beginning awaiting him. The Cubs lost badly and probably wouldn't make it to the playoffs this year. She winced, her head throbbing again, as Simon slapped the table and let out a large whoop.

"Did you see? Did you see, Anna? That was the worst loss they had all year! They haven't got a prayer of making the playoffs now!"

Noticing her wince, he became quiet and solicitous. "What's wrong, honey? Do you have another headache?" Simon worried about Anna's headaches. "You've been spending too much time at that microscope, haven't you?"

"No, not at all." Anna lied. "In fact, I don't get nearly enough time in the lab, with all the activity going on this summer. I have to make use of the student helpers while I have them; my grant money will run out soon and then I'll have to make do without helpers".

"Is there any possibility your grant will be renewed?"

Simon was concerned; he knew this project meant the world to Anna, and the preservation of this prairie was one of her top priorities. There were few enough prairies left in the world already; she didn't want to see this one lost, as well.

"No, I don't think there's any hope. I've submitted all the necessary paperwork but I don't have any real expectations the grant will be renewed. No one's concerned about biodiversity right now. It's all about the war, and all about gas prices. Most people think saving the environment is a frivolous luxury we can't afford. I really fear we'll lose this prairie soon."

Anna didn't tell Simon about the survey stakes. She didn't want to burden him with her problem, especially when she wasn't sure it really was a problem.

Simon stood behind Anna, massaging her scalp and worrying. There were a lot of changes going on in the world and he wasn't sure any of them were going to be good.

The President's speech tonight was worrisome. The president was beginning to deteriorate, both physically and mentally. During his last speech, he lapsed into something which sounded almost like speaking in tongues, a very strange thing for someone of the President's particular faith. Simon wasn't sure if that was actually what it was. Unlike Anna, he was not brought up in a church and he wasn't sure what it meant to speak in tongues. But the President was certainly speaking gibberish, no doubt about that. If they hadn't turned off the mike when they did, there's no telling what he would have said…or babbled.

The phone interrupted the quiet morning. Anna and Simon both jumped as though startled out of a reverie. Simon grabbed the phone but handed it quickly to Anna after answering. He went upstairs to get the other phone. Anna knew it must be Jason. They both got on the line when Jason called.

"Mom!"

Anna heard Jason's voice, excited, almost breathless. Jason was usually such a calm, laid back individual this in itself was startling.

"Mom, guess what? I'm getting married!"

"Married?"

Anna spoke as someone in a daze. She and Simon met the woman Jason was dating when they went to San Francisco, but Jason hadn't indicated it was serious.

"Who are you marrying?"

"Kathy, of course. You met her."

"Yes, of course, Jason. I'm sorry, I was just caught off guard for a moment. After all, it's only 7:30 a.m."

"Well, it's only 5:30 here, Mom, and I'm wide awake!"

Jason had a tone in his voice that let her know he was grinning, and wasn't upset by her absentmindedness. Anna thought "how strange Jason is up at 5:30. He's never been up at 5:30 in his life." Then Simon was on the other line and Jason filled them in on all the details. He was excited, almost too excited, Anna thought in confusion.

Finally it sank in…he's getting married. Of course he's excited. The wedding was planned for late September; she'd need to arrange to take some time from classes to attend. She really wanted to be at her son's wedding. And she liked Kathy. Kathy was a good, kind person, with a good head on her shoulders. Not like Jason, head always in the clouds. She'd be a good wife for him.

Anna hung up the phone in a daze. For the first time in her life, she was beginning to feel like she really was 50. She wasn't sure she liked it.

5

Typha logged her data entries and closed her books for the day. She wriggled out of her lab coat and left it on the hook as she closed and locked the lab door behind her. Joshua already left for the day; he rarely managed to stick it out for an entire shift, and seemed to feel his rights violated when she suggested he might work another hour.

Now that she was aware of his status as the son of an elder, she realized he considered this job beneath him, and at the same time considered it his right to have a cushy position. She expected he'd leave without making much of a mark. He'd been there two months and had as yet shown no evidence of learning even the most basic procedures. She still had to teach him each day the same things she taught him from the very beginning. In spite of the encounter today with his father, the elder, he still regarded this work as unimportant, beneath him, and something which could be folded up and left behind easily. He'd be leaving soon, she had little doubt.

His departure wouldn't bother Typha. So far, he'd been surly, uncooperative, unimaginative, lazy, and usually ended up creating more work for her than he did himself. Typha also had a nagging feeling about her own future after the encounter this afternoon. Right now she was important to the government, to the church. It was vital for them to preserve her health and her life. What if Joshua, or someone else, was able to take over?

She shivered as she remembered the dark, damp room where her mother died rather than accept the humiliation of submission to a demented dictatorship. If she had been a believer herself, Typha might have found herself mumbling a prayer as she locked the door. Instead, she gathered her daily food allotment and headed for home.

Inside her small room, TV blaring at top volume (man, how she missed the old days, when you could at least mute the sound and not have to listen to all that drivel), Typha relaxed only briefly. Although she knew it was too dangerous to risk a visit to the hideaway tonight, she needed to know what happened. There was barely an hour until the dome went dark and she needed to act fast to get a message through.

She quickly ate her tasteless dinner, Manna from Heaven they called it, swallowed the vitamin pill which kept members of the resistance healthier than the rest of the population, and slipped out the door carefully, trying to make sure no one noticed. There was one good thing about the high population density; it was easy not to be noticed among all the crowds. At this time of night, everyone was supposed to be home but there were still many people on the streets, mostly people who had no home.

There was, as always, a housing shortage. The housing shortage was chronic ever since the latter part of the last century, as the population continued to increase so rapidly the developers couldn't keep up with it. Now it was simply impossible to find more space to put anyone.

With every inch of land covered with concrete and high rise apartment buildings standing wall to wall with no space between them, it was still necessary to pack people densely into small apartments. In fact, most apartments the size of hers were home for an entire family, usually with at least six or eight children. Parents managed to make love sleeping in a double bed with most of their children, and continued reproducing in what seemed like impossible situations. They wouldn't even think of stopping; it was their duty. The lesson was drummed into their heads all their lives…their duty: reproduce, bring your children up in Christ, and perform your job diligently and without complaint. God doesn't like complainers.

Typha, brought up away from it all, her mother in charge of all her educational needs, received a different lesson. She learned about the finiteness of the earth, the reality of death, and the improbability of another life after this world. She also learned about a world which once existed, a world where there were things called trees, flowers, animals, sky, and stars.

As a child, she spent hours thumbing through the countless books handed down to her from her great-grandmother's extensive library. She read the ancient philosophers and the earliest scientists. She held in her hand a first edition of the *Origin of Species*, autographed by Charles Darwin himself, a gift from her great-grandfather to her great-grandmother shortly before the transformation.

No one today dared breathe the name Charles Darwin, if they ever happened to hear it. He was among the forbidden, listed as irredeemably evil, an instrument of darkness. Typha read Darwin eagerly, breathing in every word, unable to put the books down until she finished them all.

In the street, Typha stayed close to the wall, which wasn't difficult in the narrow alleys between the buildings. There really weren't any streets anymore; Typha had seen pictures of old times, when wide streets lined with trees were the norm in every suburb, and cities had lanes upon lanes of concrete devoted to nothing but cars.

When the population crush became overwhelming, the government desperately tried to save the highways and the cars, but the growing land shortage gained such a momentum not even the highways were safe. They, too, went extinct, bulldozed to make room for apartment houses. These buildings now provided a measure of safety for Typha as she crept along to meet a messenger for the resistance.

She needed to be careful, not so much for herself as for the resistance. She was still too important to the elders for anything other than a severe reprimand, though that was harsh enough in itself. She wouldn't be reprimanded to death; she couldn't be so confident about anyone caught meeting with her against the rules. She kept a look out on every side as she crept along the streets.

At her feet, she heard someone moan. That wasn't unusual; moaning was normal on the streets, not just at night, but all day long, as people who were temporarily or permanently without apartment space made their presence known; if they didn't, they were sure to be stepped on. This moan, however, was different. It had a cadence, not evident at first but easily picked up by her trained ear. She had stumbled, literally, onto her contact.

Leaning down as though trying to give assistance, she pressed a note into the palm of the moaning bundle. In return, she felt a crumpled piece of paper pressed into her own palm. She stood up, brushed herself off, and moved on without looking back. She didn't recognize her contact, but it was difficult to recognize anyone in the shapeless rags of the homeless which were the common mode of dress among the resistance when coming into the main city center.

Back in her apartment, alone at last, Typha leaned against the closed door and let out her breath in a long, lingering sigh. She wasn't aware of holding her breath until she released it.

The television was at its most obnoxious, tuned now to a treacly sit-com. The sit-com was nearly over; she could tell because the TV family was sitting in a circle, holding hands, ready for the prayer that ended all television shows. Another problem solved in TV time, thanks to the benevolence of the Supreme Being. The next thing up would be the news. Typha didn't want to hear the news tonight; she reached for the remote control and switched channels to one of the ubiquitous gospel music stations. News was hard to ignore; music could be shut out easily.

Typha uncrumpled the note and searched through the multiple uses to find the most current. With the trees gone, the paper mills shut down long ago. Now only the resistance had paper, and they didn't have an endless supply so they needed to make it last as long as possible. They perfected a recycling technique and were able to make their own paper from a variety of objects, but it was still very dear.

She scanned down the page, through line upon line of tiny, cramped handwriting, until she reached the line she was interested in: the one with today's date. It was only one word, but it was a word that spoke volumes: Saffron.

Typha lowered her head onto her hands and began to sob, quietly at first, then louder. An intrusion broke into her grief. Someone was knocking on her door. She brushed the tears away, ran her fingers through her hair to make it look like she'd been sleeping (that would explain the red eyes), and opened the door.

To her surprise, her neighbor to the west stood in the hallway, three kids in tow, one of them hiding behind her skirts but the other two looking boldly into her room, staring defiantly as though daring her to point out their rudeness. The mother looked...scared? Why was she scared? Behind them, the narrow hallway teemed with people, as usual full of dispossessed persons who had no where else to go.

"I thought I heard someone cryin' over here", the woman said timidly. "Is everyone all right?"

She, like her children, stared into the room, looking in vain for 'everyone'. It was a sure bet they'd never seen a room with only one person living in it before, and if they had any suspicion that she lived here alone, they must be curious as to why she wouldn't have a husband, children, or even roommates who shared with her until they found husbands.

"No, no one was crying over here", Typha lied. "I was just watching a drama on TV and I went to sleep with the TV on. There must have been some sort of sad story. I switched it to the music just now because I always like to have a little music before I go to bed."

Typha waved her hand back into the room.

"Wouldn't you like to come in?" she offered, though it was the last thing she wanted.

She couldn't afford to have her neighbors realize how different she was. The elders were very specific that no one should know she was "different". She didn't know what the penalty would be if someone found out; she didn't want to know. A cold sweat threatened to break out on her forehead as she waited for the woman to answer.

"No, I don't 'spect I'll come in tonight", the woman on her doorstep answered. "I gotta get back before my husband gets home. Is your husband still at work, dearie?"

"No, he's not."

Typha comforted herself for the lie by telling herself it wasn't, after all, really a lie. She had no husband at work. It was a semantic game she sometimes played with herself so she could manage to keep her integrity and her secret at the same time.

"It's television time", she said, somewhat stupidly to her ears, but it must have sounded all right because the neighbor nodded and moved off to her own doorway, children in tow.

Typha shut the door behind her and nearly collapsed in relief. She needed to be more careful. It wasn't just her own life that was at stake, it was the lives of everyone in the resistance. She caught sight of the crumpled paper and crumpled on the floor herself in grief. Saffron was gone. That was what it meant to just see her name. It was an epitaph.

6

Anna and Simon nestled close on the couch, wine glasses in hand, waiting for the president to arrive in the press room for his latest speech. After the near melt down last week, it was surprising his advisors were allowing him to speak again so soon. Perhaps they felt it was important for him to be seen, in control, as quickly as possible.

The tension in the room was palpable; Anna and Simon sat in a stiffer posture than they usually adopted when they cuddled together on the couch. This was going to be important and it was going to be a turning point. But which way were they turning?

Simon was nervous, but he hid his nervousness from Anna. This was new, and he didn't like it. They shared everything, especially something so important, but right now all he knew was rumors and he didn't want to create additional anxiety over rumors. The fellow in his shop today, though, said much the same thing he heard in the airport last week.

If the rumors were true, Anna was going to be distressed and he knew there wasn't much he would be able to do to help. His heart ached and he reached out to stroke her hair. She responded by leaning her head against his shoulder and stroking his arm in a way he always found stimulating. Snowball and Shadow curled on their laps, purring, and on a happier night he might have purred along with them. It could have been the picture of contentment, except for all the tension.

With a blare of *Hail to the Chief*, there was the president. He looked cool and calm, neat as usual in his well cut blue suit, smiling warmly, waving as he came into the room and took his place at the podium. A hush fell over the press corps; an unnatural hush. Everyone is nervous, Simon thought. We're all worried about what's going to happen. Or maybe we're all worried the president will have another melt down. He certainly looks calm enough.

"The time has come", the President announced, "for all Americans to pull together to protect what we care about, and what we believe in".

He was in fine form, his voice back in the familiar timbre, his rhetoric soaring above the crowd just like it did throughout the campaign two years ago. Simon dared to hope; after all, this president was all about hope.

"We have to pull together to create a stronger, healthier America, to create an America of hope instead of despair, to create an America where we feel safe in our homes, in our jobs, in our schools, and in our stores. An America where we feel safe because we're strong. And we're going to be strong again! We can be strong again!"

The crowd in the press room exploded in applause. This was what they wanted to hear…strong, positive leadership just when we needed strong, positive leadership. No more speaking in tongues. No more frightened deer in the headlights. No more fear.

"America, I call on you to do your part! It's not enough to just go shopping anymore. It's not enough to put your money on the line. I call on you to put your bodies on the line, to put your future on the line. I call on you to trust, and hope, and pray…especially to pray. And I call on you to reproduce!"

Simon sat up. This was what he'd been hearing. He heard rumors all week that the president was going to call for a massive increase in reproduction, for women to commit themselves to give birth, to go off all contraception, and to reproduce like there is no tomorrow. He heard Anna moan. He took her hand in his, and stroked it. She was shaking her head, moaning, "No, no, no."

The president was still speaking but Simon and Anna barely heard him. He was laying out a plan, a plan for reproduction, a contest pitting each of the states against all the others, to see who could increase their births the fastest.

"We can't fight against the increasing hostility around the world unless we are prepared to reverse the disturbing trends of the past few decades", the president was booming. "Women will be well compensated for their child-bearing, of course. Mothers will become even more valuable than they are already. Mothers will be cherished. We need to keep growing, for a strong economy, a strong civilization, a strong country."

"Cannon fodder", murmured Simon, "always calling for cannon fodder. And this was the president who promised to end the madness of the wars. Now he wants us to produce more cannon fodder for him".

Anna was crying uncontrollably, gasping, breathless.

"It's the wrong message", she gasped. "It's a dangerous message. It's condemning the future of the entire planet. And for what? A few minutes of glory? If that?"

24

Simon pointed at the screen. Commentators were beginning to make their analyses of the president's talk. The camera crew was stationed in Colorado Springs, the headquarters of Focus on the Family. The director stepped to the microphone, dressed neatly in an expensive black suit, well-fed and obviously soft.

It was no secret that the religious leaders of the country courted the president for some time, alternately cajoling and threatening, hoping for just such a moment. The analysis was brief and to the point. The director looked straight into the camera and broke out in a slow smile which engulfed his entire face. He held up two fingers. Vee. Victory.

"Gentlemen", he said, "this is the moment we've been waiting for. I want you to march straight into your bathroom, take your wife's pills, and flush all those nasty little things down the toilet!"

All that changed with the transformation. The transformation – the time when the spirit of the people changed. Reproduction became the highest priority for most couples, the highest expression of patriotism. Women threw away their contraceptives and left their jobs in droves as the government began paying couples large sums to have children. The population began to explode as families expanded in size, overcoming even the numbers generated in the earlier period known as "The Baby Boom".

Typha spent some time researching this phenomenon. She couldn't understand it at first, since there was no drop in population which would warrant a panic leading to non-stop reproduction. She discovered there were several things going on at the time. The United States was involved in wars on many fronts; not only throughout most of Asia, but also there were beginning to be rumblings and unrest in Africa and South America. European populations were stabilizing but many people worried that there was a "birth dearth" in Europe. Religious leaders pressed the president to put a stop to the "immorality of contraception and abortion" and declare a pro-natalist, pro-life culture.

Something else Typha learned puzzled her at first. There were numerous references in the literature of the time to the President's "conversion to Christianity". The true confusion, she realized, came from a confusion of terms. All the sources she found in the preserved materials of the time indicated the President was a Christian when he went into office.

She searched and searched to find out what this conversion was about, because none of the standard literature of the modern church acknowledged the president's Christianity upon assuming office. The conversion was a matter of dogma and it was subversive to question it. Well, Typha thought, I'm subversive. So, I think I'll ask questions. But to whom? Who could possibly know? There was no one living today who remembered the time before the transformation, or at least no one who would admit to remembering it.

Typha was still asking questions, but she'd been getting answers, and from surprising places. Most of her answers came from the computers of the elders themselves. It seems the president was what they used to refer to as a "liberal Christian". For the elders, and in the eyes of the church, this meant he wasn't a Christian. He didn't have the right belief. One night in a speech, the President was struck by the

Holy Spirit, or so the official story goes. He lost track of his speech and began speaking in tongues on national TV, to the horror of the press crews and all the people watching. His advisors shut off his mike as quickly as possible and got him out of the room. A full psychiatric exam failed to find any signs of disease and he was pronounced fit to continue as president. The next week, the president declared the new policy which, over time, would be dubbed "The Transformation".

The population explosion after the transformation wreaked havoc with the world's natural systems. Whole forests were bulldozed and concreted over for the housing of one week's worth of babies. Agricultural fields disappeared, even as more people began to make greater demands on the nation's food supply. The stress extended to the water supplies as artesian wells dried up, aquifers were overdrawn, and water tables dropped all over the country.

As the country remained distracted with wars and famines, the church made their move. All over the country, much of the social network had already been turned over to religious institutions under the belief they could do it better than secular social services. Desperate people lined up outside church food banks and water banks in lines stretching sometimes for miles. In order to get a small drink of water or a dry sandwich, people agree to be baptized even if they'd been baptized before in another church or another faith. The church ranks swelled with the masses of the hungry and thirsty.

The church had been purchasing land for years; now, it turned out, they owned most of the agricultural lands of the Midwest and anyone who wanted to eat needed to go to them. The power of the church grew until the church became the government. The elders controlled everything: every thought, every word, every deed, belonged to the church. Books burned all over the world. Only books approved by the church could be bought in bookstores or checked out at libraries. Movies and television were approved by the church until all TV became the sort of treacle that was the common fare now.

The people appealed to the church...save the environment. Save the skies, which are becoming polluted. Save the water, so we can have something to drink. The church didn't listen. They didn't need to. The church owned it all and they were leveling it at a pace unprecedented in history. Soon, they believed, they would have God's kingdom established on Earth so Jesus could return and sweep the ranks of the faithful into heaven.

The waterways dried up. The skies turned black with pollution. Grasses, trees, and flowers died, and then the animals died. Jesus didn't return and people grew increasingly desperate. The church built a dome over the Earth to protect the human species from mankind's folly. New food sources were developed, rumored to come from mineral mines in Africa, which were distributed to everyone in diminishing quantities as the population continued to grow. The food was tasteless but it kept people alive. Life expectancy dropped because the new food source didn't provide all the needed vitamins. People became pale and unhealthy. This was a danger for the resistance, who developed vitamin supplements, because they stood out, rosy-faced in a crowd of pale creatures with dead eyes.

The church discovered the need for the tissue cultures. The plants had to be kept in some form to provide oxygen. The church got rid of most scientific knowledge, considering it superfluous, but oxygen wasn't superfluous. The science books had been burned in giant conflagrations following the transformation.

The church nearly lost power in the riots when people realized the elders had executed the scientists who knew how the atmosphere worked. They'd been executed as heretics and enemies of the state. The executions were public spectacles attended by hundreds of thousands, cheering crowds who now turned against the elders, demanding air. If God's so great, they murmured, why isn't he giving us air?

The church advertised for scientists, anyone who understood plants. There were two left; they agreed to work for the government, to create oxygen, but only after long sessions with the interrogators. The scientists set up the system Typha worked with now, creating a new system from the remnants of plant material still available. The plants were grown as tissue cultures because they didn't take as much room, and provided vital gases which were vented throughout the dome which covered the entire Earth. The church once again emerged in charge.

Everywhere the church grew, the resistance grew. Small bands of men and women went underground. They took their books, their magazines, their ideas, and their children. They raised their children in a society free of the influence of the hated government, the post-transformation government, the government of God's warriors.

Typha was a child of the resistance, born underground, the child of a mother born to rebel. As she enjoyed her precious extra drink of the scarce water, she thought about the history she'd learned from her mother, from her books, and from the records of the elders. She realized she possessed something powerful, something which could work in her favor. She had history. And she had science. As long as she kept her head, and didn't let any of her interns take over control of her lab, she had hope.

8

The meeting wasn't going well. Obviously the department chair was worried; there was something on his mind other than next semester's curriculum but he didn't seem to want to talk about it. He seemed unable to focus on anything at all, and merely droned on and on about student evaluations, research grants, class schedules, and upcoming sabbaticals, without any clear direction.

The faculty shuffled their feet, growing noticeably restless; the meeting ran past the usual obligatory half hour monthly meeting and was now well into its second hour...a record, surely. One by one, the faculty crept out of the room, silently shutting the door, until at last only Anna and Harry, the chair, remained.

Anna glanced at her watch and coughed. Usually she would have been out the door with the rest, but she sensed something in the air beyond just an absent-minded professor moment. This wasn't like Harry; he ran meetings tightly to schedule, keeping them succinct, because he didn't enjoy meetings any more than the rest of the faculty. What was wrong? Harry didn't seem to notice that Anna was the only one still sitting there. He rambled on, talking about fall schedules as though the fate of the entire world depended on getting the times just right.

At the end of the second hour, the door opened and the new dean entered. Anna hadn't spoken with the new dean yet. She attended his welcoming party last week, but a crowd surrounded him and she was never introduced. She was still in shock at the abrupt resignation of the former dean, Ruth Anderson.

Ruth was still a young woman, younger than Anna, in fact, and wasn't eligible for retirement benefits. She seemed to enjoy her job and everyone expected she would remain for years. She was well liked, and most of the staff and faculty were having trouble accepting that she was gone.

Anna, a friend of hers for several years, stopped by her house after the welcome party to see how things were going. Ruth was not home, or at least her husband said she was away. Anna was pretty sure she saw Ruth look out from an upstairs window as she drove off; apparently, she wasn't prepared to talk to anyone from the school, since no one else was able to get in touch with her, either.

The new dean, Dr. Ryan, seemed efficient, but he was aloof and icy and the faculty was still adjusting to the change. Now he stood at the front of the room beside Harry, frowning at the nearly empty room.

"Where did everyone go?" Dr. Ryan asked Harry.

Harry, interrupted in mid-sentence, shook his head as though dazed and glanced around the room, noticing for the first time it was nearly empty.

"I told you to make sure the faculty was here when I got here."

Harry looked as his watch, shaking his head sadly.

"Keeping them for a two hour meeting is impossible", Harry said. "We're used to short, efficient meetings, and getting out on time. I tried to fill two hours, but it wasn't possible. I expected you earlier."

"Well, I got held up", snapped Dr. Ryan. "I was meeting with the college president and board of regents, and you don't just walk out…apparently, our faculty has no such scruples", he growled, glaring at Anna. "When I call a meeting of the faculty, I expect them to be there."

"Well, to be fair to the faculty, sir", Harry mumbled, "They didn't know you called the meeting. If you'd let me tell them you were coming…" Harry trailed off, silenced by the deepening scowl on Dr. Ryan's already unfriendly face.

"If I'd told them I was coming", Dr. Ryan roared, "They'd have found some excuse not to be here at all! Obviously, our faculty is less than totally dedicated to the mission of the university."

Noticing Anna, as if for the first time, Dr. Ryan asked Harry "Who is this? You'll have to remind me of her name".

Anna frowned at the imperialistic nature of asking Harry rather than herself. She was beginning to worry there would be a lot not to like about the new dean.

"Anna", Harry replied. "Dr. Anna Chester, one of our professors".

"Full professor?" Dr. Ryan asked.

Harry nodded. For the first time, Dr. Ryan addressed Anna herself.

"So, *Doctor* Chester, what do you teach?" The tone was condescending, almost as though speaking to a mentally retarded child.

"Botany", Anna replied. "And Ecology."

"Ah, fluff subjects", Dr. Ryan nodded. "Quite fitting for one of your delicate gender", he went on, still in a condescending tone.

Anna seethed but held her temper with effort. It wouldn't do to lash out. Let's see where all this is leading.

"Are you married?"

Anna, surprised by the question, nodded. This wasn't at all what she expected but the next question surprised her even more.

"How many children do you have, Anna?"

Boiling at the inappropriate question, and even more at the tone and the use of her first name, sans title, which reduced her to juvenile status, Anna answered cautiously, feeling her way around a potentially dangerous situation.

"One, sir", she answered with forced warmth. "One son."

"Only one?"

Anna nodded, seeing no need to state again what she'd already said perfectly clearly. It was obvious Dr. Ryan disapproved deeply.

"Are you planning to have more?" he queried.

"No, sir", Anna responded politely.

The question was more personal than she felt was appropriate but she was not yet prepared to protest.

"So why aren't you at home with your son?" Dr. Ryan asked gruffly.

"My son is 28, living in California, and married", Anna answered angrily.

This was going way beyond the bounds of appropriate questioning and she wasn't going to sit still for it any longer.

"He has a full time career in the theatre, and he is hardly in need of my mothering services at this point."

"Why aren't you planning to have more children? Don't you think you should be answering the president's call to do your patriotic duty?"

"With all due respect, sir...", Anna began, but Harry cut her off before she could answer.

"Dr. Chester has been with us a long time, Dr. Ryan, and she is older than she looks", Harry said, with less tact than he would usually employ in discussing the age of one of his employees. "She isn't at the age where she can have more children."

Turning to Anna, Harry added, in an effort to explain the strange behavior of the new dean, "Dr. Ryan is a good friend and prayer partner of the President."

Dr. Ryan sat at the head of the table with an air of self-importance. Instead of inviting Anna to close the gap between them in the casual, familiar way meetings were usually conducted on campus, as equals, Harry went to the other end of the table and sat beside Anna. The meeting took on an ominous air as Dr. Ryan shuffled papers importantly, seemingly in no hurry to explain why he called the meeting.

Anna, miffed at being treated as an infantile offender, sat silent, arms across her chest, defiant and unwilling to approach this meeting in a servile manner. She would uphold her dignity regardless of what they were planning, she vowed. She was a highly trained, respected scientist, a full professor, and with tenure…in the hard sciences, she thought to herself, as if to take the sting out of the dean's dismissal of her field as "fluff". She wasn't a wayward child, a juvenile delinquent in need of correction. So why did she feel so much like one? Anna was worried, angry, and confused.

"Perhaps you follow the news and are aware of the wonderful changes taking place in the nature of our world", Dr. Ryan began, addressing not Anna and Harry but the room in general, as though there were a large crowd hanging on his every word.

Anna began to regret feeling sorry for Harry and wished she had slipped out when the rest of the faculty did.

"We are entering a new era, an era where we restore the proper order of the world, where we establish the kingdom of God on the North American continent, to serve as a beacon to the rest of the world in hopes they will emulate our shining example and give up their sinful ways."

Anna frowned; was this really an appropriate speech for a public university dean, especially in the Science and Mathematics Department? She opened her mouth to say something but she noticed Harry shushing her anxiously. Clearly he had some idea what was going on and though he might not like it, he felt powerless to stop it.

Now Anna was really scared. In all the years she'd known him, Harry never felt powerless. He was a dynamo, super-charged, believing any problem he tackled would sooner or later (usually sooner) yield to his will. Anna sank back in her chair. This was not looking good. She remembered the speech the president gave on TV last night; he was starting to look like a fanatic and she remembered him waving his arms, the rhetoric more and more grandiose until he ended his speech on a tremendous crescendo with the exhortation to "FILL THE WORLD WITH AMERICANS!"

"We are standing at the threshold of a new era, and we have the honor of being among the generation who will usher in the best of all worlds. In this world, there will be no room for the cult of the individual, the idea that we are sufficient unto ourselves, or that we know better than the greater society. This will be an era where all of us work together to make the world a testament to glory. Our university has pledged to do their part, and to bring our faculty, staff, and students into the new order of things as quickly as possible. I know that all of you...", here Dr. Ryan broke off, looked around at the nearly empty room, and frowned..."all of you are thrilled to be part of the new system. I know I can count on all of you to do your part to ensure a smooth transition to the new society that lies ahead."

Dr. Ryan began to lay out the new plans for the school. All female students would be immediately diverted into a more suitable program; they would no longer be admitted to science and math, as those programs were not considered appropriate to meeting the overall goal of enhancing reproduction. All the women science students would be moved into a new program called Childcare for Homemakers.

The school only intended to run this program for a generation, as it was only deemed necessary for the retraining of the current female generation who were improperly raised to believe there were other roles which might be considered appropriate for women. After that, Dr. Ryan explained, there would be no need of admitting women to the schools at all, because mothers would raise their daughters correctly, like they used to, with an understanding of the proper role for young women: marry young and fulfill their glorious future as a mother.

Anna listened but she had trouble believing what she heard. She was breathing so shallowly and rapidly, she began to worry she was hyperventilating. Her whole body quivered with anger.

"As for the female faculty", Dr. Ryan continued, "We'll allow them to retire quietly, giving them a stipend for the remainder of their childbearing years. Those who are no longer of childbearing age", he looked pointedly at Anna as he said this, as if doubting the truth of Harry's statement "will be allowed to continue in their positions until we find a suitable replacement. This is an area we haven't totally worked out yet, as we hadn't realized we had so many women on the faculty, and so many women who are…post-menopausal."

The last word he spat out with contempt, as though there were some crime committed by women who reached an age where they were no longer able to bear children. Anna had a sudden, strange realization that in the new order of things, they were indeed criminals, rendered felonious by the natural aging of their own bodies. The day grew dark and chilly though it was obvious the sun was still shining outside.

When Anna got back to her office, she found the rest of the faculty crowded in the faculty lounge, staring in disbelief at a large announcement taped over the copy machine. This announcement served to let everyone know what they missed by not remaining at the meeting. Joining the crowd, Anna read the announcement, realizing it was nearly word for word the same as the speech the dean just delivered to his truncated audience.

There was none of the babbling or griping which usually accompanied an announcement of a policy change; the entire science faculty stood in uncharacteristic, stunned silence. No one moved, no one spoke. Anna felt like she was in one of those movies where all the characters freeze except one, and she was the one. Reaching up to the bulletin board, she ripped the announcement off the wall and boldly tore it in two.

The sound of ripping paper brought the faculty back to life and the room filled with the usual chatter that accompanied unpopular policy changes. Within moments, a resistance formed, led by Anna but with support from everyone else. For the first time in months, perhaps years, this usually divisive and competitive faculty appeared to operate as one body. The group elected Anna president of a newly formed "Faculty Coalition" and made plans for campus-wide organization. Following a short, 15-minute meeting, the group roused to action, made plans for fighting back, and deployed the phones to rouse colleagues in other departments all over campus.

It soon became evident the new plan was no more popular anywhere else than it was in their department…except in the newly formed Childcare for Homemakers program, which cheered the new policy lustily. Anna, as official representative of the Biology faculty, broke from the ranks to attend a hastily organized campus-wide Faculty Coalition meeting in the library, where librarians joined the resistance and reserved a large meeting room for the faculty and staff representatives.

As she and Simon nestled on the couch after dinner, Anna shared the events of the day. Simon was caught off guard, though he did acknowledge he received a strange memo at his shop from the Chamber of Commerce, of which he was a member. He said he was given some rather cryptic instructions that he should politely inquire of any female employees about their marital status, number of children, and future plans for childbearing. He received a form to fill out and return, which he promptly tore into tiny bits, shoved into an envelope with a strong letter about the illegality of such inquiries, and mailed it back to the Chamber, COD.

Simon had no intention of violating the privacy of his employee, though he could easily have told them the one elderly woman who worked part time in his shop was not planning on bearing any more children. The policy changes at the school, however, went deeper than the mere intrusion into the personal lives of his personnel.

Even with all the changes over the past several months, Simon preferred to believe this was all a passing bit of nonsense which would soon blow over as soon as everyone came back to their senses. Like Anna, he noticed the increasing fanaticism of the President's rhetoric and he was equally concerned at the command to fill the world with Americans, but he tended to think it was the usual overblown, out of perspective rhetoric which had characterized American politics for the past several decades.

Now he wasn't so sure. He was worried. Worried about the future of the country, the future of the planet, and worried, most of all, about Anna. He was right behind her all the way in her brave stand, and he knew she wouldn't be afraid to stand up for what she believed. He also knew, deep down, she had nothing to lose.

Recent events suggested that, in the absence of the resistance, she had no chance of retaining the life she struggled and worked so hard to achieve. It wasn't the possibility of losing her job which had him worried because she was probably already in line for termination, given the new policy. He was worried she would lose her dignity, which was something he knew she would never be able to bear.

Besides, she was already so overworked and stressed out, with her efforts to protect the environment from further damage, he wasn't sure how much more she could take on.

He vowed to cherish her even more than he already did, if such a thing was possible, and he vowed he would take as much work as possible off her shoulders to allow her to get a little rest from time to time. He squeezed her hand in solidarity and felt rewarded as she flashed him the beautiful smile he always looked forward to.

"I'll be right beside you", he whispered, as he stroked her hair. "I'll always be beside you."

9

Typha was restless. For the past couple of weeks, she hadn't been able to get out of her apartment to see her friends because of the clamp down. She avoided the services the resistance held for Saffron because of the risk of being followed and unintentionally betraying still more of her friends. Surrounded on all sides by so many people she couldn't leave her room without nearly walking on them, she still felt lonely. No, it wasn't really lonely, was it? It was something...different.

She lay back on her bed, hands behind her head, and thought about Aspen. When was the last time they were together? It must have been at least two months since they were able to sneak a few minutes of clandestine time, and she missed him. She longed to get lost in the mysterious depths of his deep hazel eyes, feel the touch of his hand on her hair, nestle her head against his chest. It was difficult being apart all the time, but she realized in her current job she was in a better position to be of use to the resistance than when she lived in their midst, one of them totally.

She didn't feel like being noble. She felt like being selfish, and she allowed herself a few moments of rare self-pity. She did worry that, with her so far away, Aspen might find someone else who appealed to him and was near by, someone who could fill his needs when she wasn't around. She frowned, clenched her fists by her side, and put it out of her mind. She believed Aspen was loyal but she couldn't dwell on the possibility. If he didn't stay with her, she'd have to deal with the pain when it happened. She needed to keep her spirits up so she wouldn't let down her guard and do something foolish. She thought about Saffron. Saffron, and Spider, and Turnip, and Riata, and Java...all the ones who'd fallen in the fight. She owed it to them, to all of them, and more. She owed it to her mother.

She first met Aspen when she was fifteen. He showed up one morning unannounced at the meeting place. Nobody knew him. He was from far away and he was not raised a rebel. Aspen wasn't his real name; when they first met him he was Caleb, but he wanted to get away from his past, to lay aside his biblically inspired name and select a new name, a resistance name. He selected the name Aspen from one of the travel books in the library.

Aspen was eighteen at the time and Typha could never get enough of listening to his stories. The family Aspen was born into devoutly believed in the philosophy of the transformation. He was one of seventeen children living in a three bedroom apartment in Fargo, North Dakota. North Dakota was one of the least densely populated states, with only 1000 people per square mile; in spite of that, Aspen felt crowded by the mobs of people surrounding him on all sides as he ate, drank, slept, and went to school.

Like most children, he was taught to read by his church, reading only approved church literature. He cooperated in every way most of his youth, until one day, walking home from church, he met an old man reading a book which wasn't approved by the authorities. And in broad daylight! Aspen was curious and approached him cautiously, remembering what he'd been taught about people who refuse to conform to the proper way of living.

He wasn't sure why he approached him, but something seemed to draw him. The old man barely looked up when Aspen sat next to him; he was engrossed in the book. Aspen glanced at it sideways, trying to look like he wasn't looking. The book was obviously old, the pages yellow and brittle. The print seemed small and cramped, not like the large print easy-to-read books he was used to reading. The title was curious, too. It was called "The Voyage of the Beagle" and was written by someone called Charles Darwin.

Typha got excited; she read a lot of Darwin, and she owned a copy of the book he was talking about. The works of Darwin were an important part of her mother's collection, passed down to Typha from her great-grandmother.

The old man, Aspen continued, noticed him looking at the book and seemed to guess he was curious, and to understand he wasn't sent by the elders. They began talking, and after about a half hour he invited Aspen to see the rest of his books, in the hiding place where he stashed them.

They went to a secret underground storage site, and Aspen couldn't believe his eyes. Wall upon wall of books, in many languages, covered nearly every surface. There must have been hundreds of books, maybe even thousands. The old man explained that when the transformation occurred he was still a young man, not yet in his teens. He grew up in a family where reading was taken for granted. Every evening after dinner, the family sat and read together instead of watching television.

Aspen struggled to understand. How could you not watch television? It isn't possible to turn it off, even if you wanted to, and why would you want to? Everything was on television....news, entertainment, everything you could possibly want. The old man explained a lot to Aspen, all about how it was before the transformation when television was optional and people could choose not to watch.

Back then, the old man said, books were easily available and they didn't have to be approved by the church or the government. People were free to write about whatever topic they wanted...they could write fantasy or horror, science fiction or romance, westerns or period novels. And non-fiction, as well...religion, science, politics, animals, whatever you might be interested in.

Whenever Aspen told the story, he usually stopped here for effect. Then he went on. "Animals?" he'd say, mimicking his own perplexity from his oblivious youth. "What is animals? I've never heard of that?" He loved to tell the story of how the old man raised his arm and he ducked, thinking he was about to be hit for asking a question. But the old man was just reaching for a book on the shelf above his head.

He pulled it down and thumbed through it until he found just what he wanted. He placed it in front of Aspen. Aspen could remember to this day what the page was...it was a picture of a gorilla. Staring in wonder, Aspen reached for the book. The picture was accompanied by text explaining the biology of the gorilla and Aspen read it eagerly, much like a starving man wolfing down food. This was a whole new thing for him. Why hadn't his teachers told him about this? Where are these animals? Where could he see one? He really wanted to see a gorilla first hand.

The old man shook his head sadly. There are no more gorillas, he explained. The last gorilla went extinct many years ago. They were already in trouble even before the transformation; the transformation finished what had already started, crowding them out of what little habitat they had remaining. With populations in the savannah in the hundreds of thousands per acre, there wasn't a single spot left for a gorilla...or anything else.

Aspen sank to his knees at this point in the story to demonstrate his reaction when he learned this. He started to cry, though he wasn't sure why. He felt like he just lost something he cherished, even though he'd only heard about gorillas a minute or two before. He looked at the picture and realized…the gorilla was looking at him with eerily human-like eyes, almost like a really hairy man.

Aspen was hooked. He went to visit the old man regularly, any chance he had when he could get away without being seen. From the old man he learned another side of the transformation, a side vastly different from the glorious, triumphant story he was taught in his sanctuary school.

The old man, he learned, was part of a resistance movement which remained underground most of the time, working against the elders, attempting to subvert their purposes. He was sitting on the park bench the day he met Aspen as part of that subversion, looking for someone to recruit to take his place, to be willing to work for restoration of a sane society.

Aspen knew meeting the old man was dangerous, not just to him but to the entire resistance movement, so he had to be careful. He always slipped away with the greatest care, and spent as many afternoons as possible in the storage site, reading books as rapidly as he could. Some of them were hard going; old technical manuals, science textbooks, mathematics…all sorts of knowledge he'd never been given, because in the current society it was assumed no one would ever need to know those things again and they were considered highly dangerous. He learned a lot from the old man and began to regard him as a grandfather.

One day when Aspen left home to go visit the old man, he got the sense he was being followed. He'd planned for this contingency and mapped out a circuitous route in advance, a route which would lead anyone following him far away from the old man and his hidden room. After looping around several times, he turned right and ended up right in front of the sanctuary school, where he had told his parents he was going to be spending the afternoon.

He went inside and leafed through the simplistic books on the tables. The man following him stood nearby, and another man who entered immediately afterward took up a position on the other side. Aspen spent an hour at the sanctuary, and when he left he took a straight path home.

He knew he wouldn't be able to visit the old man that day. At dinner, as the family was eating their mineral manna, the television blaring loudly as usual, his father casually dropped the news that the elders rounded up a dangerous subversive early in the morning, an old man who sat around on park benches reading forbidden books in an attempt to lure young people into disobedience to the authorities.

"Unfortunately", his father said, "the interrogators weren't able to get him to reveal the name of his current young recruit. They know there is someone but they're not sure who. They had a suspect, they told me, but they followed him all day and he didn't go anywhere but the church. The old man didn't survive interrogation, unfortunately, so they're going to have to figure out some other way to discover his recruit."

Aspen felt sure he must have gone pale, but the family didn't seem to notice. His parents kept talking about the dangerous subversive old man and his brothers and sisters weren't interested. They were only interested in the tepid comedy being played out on the television screen.

Aspen wanted to excuse himself but didn't dare. To not sit with the family in the evening would look suspicious. Besides, where would he go? With nineteen people in their small apartment, there wasn't a single spot a person could go for solitude. The only time in his life he ever experienced solitude and quiet was in the hidden rooms of the old man. According to his father, the authorities emptied out his hiding place, burned all his books, and destroyed every trace of the resistance they could find. Aspen felt a deep sense of loss as though he lost not only the old man, but also as though they had destroyed the last remaining gorilla.

Aspen knew there was no choice; he had to leave. Now that he knew about the world before the transformation, now that he'd read all the things in those books, he wasn't able to just go back to his old life. He knew there wasn't much chance for him to get away safely but he had to try. Late in the evening, after curfew, he slipped out of the apartment, careful not to step on any of the homeless lining the streets, and left Fargo forever.

The old man told him the heart of the resistance was centered out of a place called Ames, Iowa, and he headed in the direction he believed was correct. It took him nearly a year to get there, because he needed to lay low a lot of the time to avoid the elders who sent their troops looking for him. One of the good things about the population explosion was the ease with which a single individual could hide from the elders; because every bit of space was occupied by human habitation and so densely populated, it was easy to get lost in a crowd. Of course, since all the cities ran into each other and there was no clearly demarcated area between the cities, it could be somewhat difficult to keep up with where you were, so he got lost several times on the way. Eventually he turned up in the nerve center of the resistance, which was where they found him.

Typha loved Aspen; she loved him from the first moment she saw him. At first there was the risk he was a plant, so everybody was cautious around him. She knew if he turned out to be a plant, he could never be allowed to leave alive because he'd already seen too much. She took her turn watching him when he first showed up, nervously, because he might be dangerous and because she was afraid he might see she loved him.

Shy and quiet, Typha typically said little on her watch. About a week after his arrival, Aspen surprised her by asking her if she'd ever heard of gorillas. She told him yes, she was familiar with gorillas, and also with chimpanzees and orangutans. He asked if she had any books on the topic, and Typha fetched several volumes about primates, including a handful of books on human evolution.

They discussed apes and monkeys for hours; Aspen never had the opportunity to speak with someone so knowledgeable about biology before. The old man was a wonderful source of information but his chief interest was astronomy. He spent many hours lost in studying the stars; he hadn't spent nearly as much time on biology.

Typha and Aspen became fast friends and she taught him a lot about science. She also taught him about the resistance. He was amazed at the amount of knowledge such a young girl had of the world, but he soaked up everything she could teach him. He was ashamed of spending his youth watching television, but of course, he'd never been introduced to such things until he was fifteen himself.

Aspen grew to love Typha as much as she loved him and he looked forward to their time together as eagerly as she did. When Typha and her mother were captured by the elders and handed over to the interrogators, Aspen thought his world would come to an end if anything happened to her. After her mother died, Aspen was the only one who could provide any comfort. Over time the relationship deepened and when she was nineteen, they became lovers.

Typha ached for Aspen now. She hadn't seen him in weeks and she longed for the sweetness of his touch, the feel of his warm breath on the back of her neck. She tossed and turned, unable to get comfortable.

The dream was a familiar one, frequently interrupting her rest with terrifying images. She and her mother were on the run again, eluding the elders but eventually captured. When her mother was dying in the interrogation room, her face became indistinct and unclear; it morphed into Aspen's face, contorted in the last moments into a fearsome death mask.

Typha woke up shivering although the temperature was constantly controlled at 75 degrees over night. She shook off the last traces of sleep and sat up in bed, thirsty. She had saved a tiny bit of her water allotment for the middle of the night. Sipping it slowly to savor the rare wetness, she pulled the thin blanket around her thin shoulders and hunched over in despair. It was difficult to go on at times like these and she wondered how her mother managed for so long.

Typha couldn't get back to sleep. Reaching under her bed, she extracted the book hidden in a secret pocket in the bottom of the mattress. The light was out for the night, the dome dark and silent, but she had a small stash of candles she used sparingly for times like this. The candles were left over contraband from pre-transformation days and they doled them out in limited numbers as needed. She kept a small booklet of matches stashed in the pocket with the candle. She huddled in the small bed, candlelight flickering with a sickly yellow flame, and began to read: "It was the best of times, it was the worst of times". This time, Charles Dickens had gotten it only half right.

10

Anna screamed, waking Simon. It was the same nightmare, the nightmare which had become a recurrent theme in the past few weeks.

She and Simon were on the run from something…someone…she couldn't tell what. It was dark and they were running out of energy. She stumbled and fell; Simon stopped to help her and the pursuers were on them. They were taken to a grim building, where they were strapped into chairs she recognized as electric chairs from pictures she'd seen. On their heads were death masks, like the ones in National Geographic photo spreads.

She looked for Simon but couldn't see him because a fog rose between them, blocking him from her vision. She could hear him. He was arguing, protesting, refusing to answer questions. She heard him moan and the fog lifted. The death mask he wore was covered with tears, bloody tears, and his body slumped at an unnatural angle.

The person – was it a person? – standing over him held some sort of sinister looking tool, its exact use unclear, but she could tell it couldn't be good. The face of the tormenter was covered with a white sheet and on his head he wore the Pope's hat. He directed the tool to Simon's genitals, eliciting a deep moan.

It was always at this point Anna awoke, sometimes with a scream. She shuddered in the cold darkness, relieved to feel Simon's arms holding her, comforting her.

"Shhh, it was just a dream. You'll be all right. I'm right here."

He talked to her in the same tone of voice they used to talk to Jason when he was little and had a bad dream or was scared of a thunderstorm. Anna curled inside Simon's arms like a tiny kitten, scared and shivering but enjoying the warmth of his embrace. Simon held her for half an hour until she fell asleep again. Then he rolled over on his back, hands behind his head, and lay awake in the dark until morning, a silent vigil, thinking, worrying. Worst of all was the feeling of helplessness.

Anna rose early. It was Saturday and she allowed Simon to sleep in. She called the store at nine. Doris opened up and the store was running smoothly. Anna told her to go ahead and close the store at noon, like usual. She didn't know if Simon would be in or not, because he wasn't feeling well. Doris agreed cheerfully; she was really a treasure of an employee and Simon felt lucky to have had her as an employee for so many years.

Simon woke late and came downstairs to see Anna still seated at the breakfast table. She made him a full breakfast, just like in the old days when he didn't work on Saturdays. She looked up at him with forced cheerfulness, the smile on her face belied by the bleak look in her eyes.

"Good morning, sunshine. I've got coffee on for you, and there's orange juice cooling in the fridge. Sit down and join me for an omelet."

Simon couldn't refuse. Anna's omelets were spectacular and he attacked it with gusto. They ate breakfast in silence, their usual morning conversation blunted by the terrors of the night. No matter how hard they tried, it was impossible to pretend things were normal.

The phone rang and Anna rushed to answer. Jason's voice was worried and frightened, his words tumbling over one another as if he couldn't get them out fast enough.

"Mom, something terrible is going on. Kathy's been arrested!"

"Arrested? For what?"

Anna was shocked. Kathy was a sweet girl, not capable of hurting a fly, nor breaking the law. It was hard to imagine anything she could have done to get her arrested.

"I don't know. The FBI came by this morning and took her. It was very early…about 3:00. I've been calling all over, trying to figure out where she's been taken, but I haven't been able to get any answers. I can't imagine what's going on…." Jason broke off… "Can you hold on a minute?"

Anna nodded, then realized Jason couldn't see her nod over the phone. He was gone for less than a minute before she heard his voice again.

"Kathy's home. I'll call you back in a couple of minutes, okay?"

Anna murmured her assent. "We'll be here all morning", she told him.

Simon was stunned. He only heard Anna's side of the conversation but that was enough to worry him. Anna explained the peculiar situation, and they perched nervously on the couch trying to read the morning paper, waiting for Jason to call back. The call wasn't long in coming. Simon snatched the phone before Anna could reach across him.

"What's going on, son?" Simon asked.

Anna couldn't tell from his face what he was hearing but she could tell it was bad. His face got redder and redder and Anna began to worry he was going to have a stroke. He turned to Anna and thrust the phone at her.

"He wants to talk to you. Try to keep your cool, sweetheart. It's not going to be easy."

Anna heard Jason's voice but it didn't sound like Jason, usually so carefree and lighthearted. This was a new Jason, scared and confused, his voice tight with emotion.

"Kathy got picked up because she isn't pregnant", he told her. "She's using birth control because we aren't planning on having children until we've been married a few years. When they questioned her on our plans, she told them we only planned to have one. They told her that was unacceptable and she would have to reconsider her decision. She told them she'd have to talk with me about it because, after all, I'm the other partner in the marriage, and she felt I should have some say. Apparently that was the right thing to say and it gained her some time, as they released her to my custody. They told her she's not allowed to go anywhere, even to work, without my permission. What the hell is all this about?"

Jason's voice got tighter as he told the story.

"Just a minute, okay?" he said, and Anna heard him speak to someone, probably Kathy, in the background. "Mom?"

"I'm still here."

"Kathy wants to talk to you, okay?"

"Sure, Jason. Put her on."

Anna heard Kathy pick up the other phone. Good, they were both going to be on the line. She needed to talk to both of them at once.

"Mom?" Kathy said. Her voice was small and frightened, not her usual confident, cheerful voice. "Mom, are you there?"

"I'm here, sweetie", Anna told her.

"Mom, I'm scared. I don't know what to do. I don't understand what's going on."

"I think it has something to do with the new policy the president announced last fall." Anna selected her words carefully. "You know, the one they're calling the transformation."

"I thought that was strictly voluntary", Kathy said. "I didn't know they were requiring us by law to have lots of children. Jason

48

and I just want one, and not right away. Besides, I think it's a bad plan to bring so many children into a world that's already overpopulated. I don't like this. And if birth control is against the law, how come I can still obtain it at the pharmacy?"

Anna wished she had answers for Kathy, but she wasn't able to figure it out either. She knew Kathy didn't expect her to know the answers but needed someone to talk to, so she listened. Kathy told her everything about the experience with the FBI. They were on the phone for over an hour.

"Kathy, Jason, listen to me. I want you to get plane tickets as soon as you can, and come home to Ames. I know you have your work and you're trying to get a play produced, but I think we need to talk this out in person. I think it's time we began a systematic resistance to the new regulations, rather than just the scattered, random responses we're currently involved in. See if you can get a plane out this afternoon or tomorrow morning. I'll pick you up at the airport."

Cautiously, as though it were a dangerous weapon, Anna laid the phone back on the cradle. She stood in the middle of the living room trying to grasp the enormity of what was happening. Shaking herself to clear her head, she turned to Simon.

"Jason and Kathy are coming. We need to prepare Jason's old room for them. At least the FBI told Kathy she could leave as long as she has Jason's permission."

11

Typha was breaking in a new assistant. Joshua hadn't been in for at least a week, and she found out he decided the job was too low for him if it was something a woman was able to do. She didn't care. She was glad to see him go.

Her new assistant, David, had a sunny disposition and seemed eager to learn. He also seemed to have a quick intellect, which was definitely a plus, though his quick learning made Typha nervous. The last thing she wanted was for someone to be able to do her job well enough to make her superfluous.

David was friendly and tried hard to pull the shy Typha into conversation. He seemed to want to get to know her, but Typha had been part of the resistance her whole life, and was careful not to let anyone get to know too much.

"Typha. That's an unusual name", David said on his first morning. "Not Biblical, surely?"

"No, not Biblical", Typha answered cautiously.

"I didn't think anyone had non-Biblical names. At least, no one living outside the underground", David said. "I was named after King David", he said proudly.

"Yes, I know all about King David", Typha said. "I've read the Bible, and studied it extensively."

Her admission was a little incautious, she realized after she said it. Most people didn't read the *entire* Bible, only those parts the elders considered important and appropriate. David didn't seem to notice.

"So, what does Typha mean, anyway?"

"Actually, it's a type of...", Typha trailed off.

She almost said something subversive, and right now she was trying to lay low. She'd almost gotten picked up last week on a sneak visit to see Aspen. She needed to be more careful or she would jeopardize everyone's safety.

"A type of...what?" David asked curiously.

"Oh, just a type of name that doesn't mean anything in particular. It's a family name", Typha lied.

Well, it wasn't totally a lie. She'd been named Typha by her botanist mother, who was particularly amused to name her daughter after the cattail, one of the plants that had been a particular favorite of her great-grandmother. Typha knew she couldn't tell anyone outside the resistance the meaning of her name.

Even mentioning plants was considered a subversive idea. Ever since the plants and animals went extinct, it was forbidden to mention they ever existed. Such a simple comment might be taken as an admission that living things once existed which didn't exist anymore. It might be seen as an accusation of failure on the part of the elders, and criticism of the church wasn't allowed.

The elders burned all books which mentioned living organisms other than humans, particularly those with pictures, so there wouldn't be any risk of people becoming discontent, wishing they could see these strange and interesting species. Wiped out of existence, and wiped out of memory.

Typha thought about all the wonderful picture books, all the old field guides, all the old biology textbooks stashed in the secret hiding place, and all the wonderful organisms she would never have a chance to see. She felt like crying but she choked back her tears and went about her work. She wiped away the one tear that escaped down her cheek, apparently unnoticed by her new assistant.

David didn't press her for further information, but watched her quick hands move delicately across the instruments. He was impressed, even though he knew better than to say so, at least not yet. He'd never known anyone like Typha and his curiosity was piqued. Who was this woman, working in an area where women typically weren't allowed to work? Where had she learned all the things she knew? Why was such a pretty little thing unmarried?

David hummed as he worked. There would be time to get to know all about Typha. He hoped to be working here for a very long time. He was loving every minute of it. He'd found his place. He glanced sideways at Typha from time to time, wondering if he'd also found his wife. For the first time in his life he'd actually met a woman who was not only attractive, but intelligent, educated, and interesting to talk to. Where did she get so educated? Why were her cheeks so much rosier than the pale cheeks of all the other women he knew?

He made a mental note to find out all he could about this shy, mysterious woman with the soft red hair and the flashing green eyes. Meanwhile he focused his attention on learning how to vent the oxygen out of the plant lab into the main dome. After all, he wouldn't be able to find out much about her if he failed at his job. David found himself humming a jaunty hymn as he worked side by side with the woman he was sure he was beginning to fall in love with.

12

Jason slumped in the seat, his usual joy and energy drained as he watched his mother maneuver the car through the labyrinth of the airport parking lot. If anything could have made him feel more worried and upset than he already did, it was the sight of his vivacious and energetic mother uncharacteristically glum, and the large black bags under her eyes. Her eyes were reddened from lack of sleep...or had she been crying?

Jason couldn't be sure. He only knew she didn't look like herself, and her voice trembled with an unfamiliar emotion. He wrapped her in his usual bear hug, and felt her arms wrap around him like a drowning woman holding on to a lifeguard. It wasn't unlike yesterday morning, when Kathy held him like she'd never be able to let go after the FBI dropped her at their door.

If he'd hoped for comfort from his mother's presence, it seemed it wasn't going to be forthcoming. He frowned as he watched his mother greet his wife, the two women unusually joyless. He sank into his seat and wrestled with his darkening thoughts. The women were also silent, lost in some tormented world from which he couldn't rescue. This was bigger than all of them, and for the first time in his life Jason felt afraid of the future.

Kathy watched the countryside go by, unfamiliar countryside, with huge fields of something...was it corn?...stretching as far as the eye could see. Funny, she thought, she traveled all over the world but she'd never been here, in the interior of her own country. Coast to coast travel was so easy, she'd always just flown over this area and never paid much attention to it.

She and Jason had meant to visit his home several times but always seemed to be too busy. When she finally visited, it was in a moment of conflict and fear. She hadn't wanted her first visit to be this way. She was fond of Jason's parents, who seemed like special people. She knew they had to be as special as they seemed because they raised such a special son.

She glanced at Jason lovingly, but his face looked like that of a stranger, so closed and distant, so...afraid. She'd never seen Jason afraid before. He always faced life fearlessly, confident of his own ability to overcome any obstacle. Kathy, too, was unaccustomed to fear and she was exhausted by the weight of it.

She snuggled close to Jason and his arm went around her. Comforted by the familiar gesture, she nestled in his arms and fell asleep, drained by the emotional events of the past few days. Jason smiled at the top of her head, cherishing the tangle of red hair, and somehow the normality of his sleeping wife comforted him. He, too, fell asleep as the car moved smoothly over the highway toward home.

Anna glanced in the rearview mirror at the sleeping couple. She was glad they were getting some sleep; the hollowness of their eyes startled her when she met them at the airport. She wasn't aware of the impact of her own drained, exhausted face. She was so concerned about Kathy, she hadn't noticed the startled look on Jason's face as he caught sight of her dead eyes and the pallor which had become her new color. By the time she turned to Jason, he managed to control his reaction with the aplomb that came naturally to a professional actor and he appeared to be his hearty self again, though to his mother the heartiness rang hollow.

She still couldn't get over the fear she heard in his voice on the phone, a fear as unfamiliar in Jason as it was in Simon…or in herself, for that matter. Fear had not been a common emotion in their family, at least not a fear so overwhelming it left them feeling powerless.

Anna straightened her shoulders in determination as she expertly steered the car over the road; she was not powerless. No, she wouldn't let this beat her, though at times it seemed impossible to do otherwise. She was taking action, and her friends and colleagues were right beside her. This president was elected by a democratic process; he could certainly be overruled by the same democratic process.

Anna thought about the hectic activity of the past couple of weeks. Ever since the meeting with the dean, things moved fast. The Faculty Coalition made contacts with other faculty all over the country and they now had a network of resistance to the new policies being announced in every public school. The nationwide network was headquartered in their department, and Anna was the *de facto* head of the national group.

It was a lot of work, in addition to everything else she was involved in, but she was determined to do the coalition justice. There were reductions in her workload, of course, as a result of the reassignment of all her graduate students.

Her female graduate students were moved against their will to the Childcare for Homemakers program. Her male graduate students were reassigned to a male mentor, since the new policy did not allow female instructors to hold authority over males, whether students or instructors.

Anna fired off a strongly worded letter of protest under the authority of the nationwide coalition, and the NEA was working with the ACLU on a class action lawsuit filed on behalf of the female teachers and students, as well as the male students, none of whom wanted to be reassigned. Anna was proud of the letter, in which she referenced the "newly resurgent medieval value system that served to subordinate half the human race based solely on discredited theories of inherent inferiority based on chromosomal differences between the genders". Thinking about the coalition made Anna feel better, and she hummed as she pulled into the driveway.

Jason and Kathy woke up as the car came to a halt, feeling guilty because they hadn't stayed awake and visited with Anna. They had seen her only briefly several months ago at their wedding and hadn't had a chance to visit since. There was a lot of catching up to do, and they slept like babies all the way home, leaving her to think about their problems in silence. Anna assured them she was happy they were able to get a little sleep, because no doubt they would need all the rest they could get. The fight to restore order and sanity was going to require a lot of strength.

Simon made lunch and they all sat down to a light meal of grilled cheese sandwiches, coleslaw, and milk. The talk was light during lunch by an unspoken understanding, just catching up on the day to day happenings in Jason and Kathy's world. Jason told Anna and Simon about his latest project, and Kathy filled them in on a class she was teaching at the local YWCA for aspiring 8-year-old actresses. For a short time the world returned to normal and everybody forgot the escalating lunacy of the current political scene.

13

Typha sighed with relief as the news came to an end and the television clicked off just in time for lights out. The news depressed her this week, with constant coverage of the Transnational Conference on Population Expansion going on in Geneva. With so many people in the world there wasn't food, water, or space enough for them all, but the world leaders were still concerned the population wasn't expanding fast enough!

The constant babies race all the countries were involved in had expanded the population beyond the limits of the earth's capacity to support them, leading to annual death rates in the billions, but still there were calls for more and more babies. This year's winner of the baby race was Germany. Germany won for the past three years in a row, out-producing even the United States and Nigeria who for the past several decades dominated the sweepstakes in alternating years.

The president of the World Population Conference, Leah Rachel Christianson, praised the newly fecund Germans, noting that they had more than compensated for their short period of negative population growth during the end of the 20th century into the early 21st century.

"Never again will we see Germany failing to pull their own weight in the fertility market", Christianson said. "Germany has seen the light, and realizes that, when it comes to being fruitful and multiplying, quantity trumps quality every time. Welcome back to the human race, Germany!"

Typha groaned, put her hands over her ears, and stuffed her head under her pillow. The sound of the news filled the small room, unable to be switched off except by turning to an even more vapid and disgusting situation comedy, a mindless game show, or a formulaic heartwarming drama where good Christian parents raised whole armies of identical, obedient Christian children. The entertainment channels were even harder to bear than the news. She wasn't in the mood for gospel music tonight.

Now it was silent and she could read by candlelight before she retired. The candles were limited so she wouldn't be able to read for long, but at least it was finally quiet enough for her to comprehend the written words on the page.

This week she was reading a classic novel, *Candide*, by a French writer named Voltaire. She was told by someone in the network that this was the last remaining copy of this work, so she turned the brittle yellow pages with exaggerated care and held the candle as far away from the page as possible to avoid dripping wax on the precious words.

Typha sat up straight. She just had a wonderful idea. Why hadn't anyone thought of it before? She stared intently at the words on the page, eerie in the dancing candlelight, idly thinking about the original writers of all the books stored deep underground. She imagined Voltaire, sitting at his writing desk in the 18th century, perhaps writing by candlelight himself as the shadows fell, unable to cut off his muse with the coming of darkness.

As the image passed through her mind, she began to see changes in the face of the Frenchman until the face eventually morphed into her mother's face and gradually into her own. That's it! There's no reason the writings can't be preserved just because the paper is old and brittle and the remaining copies are disintegrating in the hands of those reading them, or are being discovered and destroyed by the authorities.

There's no reason, she repeated to herself, for the literature to die out. We can copy it. We can make new editions of the old works to ensure their eternal existence. Typha practically shouted with joy at the idea. Why hadn't anyone thought of it before? Why hadn't her mother? Her mother always seemed to think of everything, the answer to all the problems. Why hadn't she thought of this?

Typha could hardly wait to pass her idea on to the resistance. She slipped out of her room, stepping carefully over the bodies of the currently homeless lining the hallways and stairs, down the six flights of stairs, and out into the darkness.

Whistling silently, she headed due east toward the rising sun, though the rising sun could no longer be seen through the dome. For the first couple of decades of her life, the elders tried to simulate the rising of the sun in the morning and they provided artificial twinkling lights to simulate stars at night. The practice died out, partially because of labor and expense, and partially because the elders found it distracting to have people questioning what happened to the original sun and the original stars.

The night now was dark and moonless, because people weren't supposed to be out after curfew anyway. The darkness suited Typha; it was easier to hide her progress through the streets. With so many bodies crammed together in the narrow streets, coupled with total lack of illumination, it was difficult for the police or the army to spot a person out walking…if the slow creeping progress through the swarming humans, trying to avoid stepping on anyone, could truly be called walking.

In record time, Typha reached one of the hidden entrances to the resistance hideaway. She was adept at finding these obscure spots in the darkness, and she used her secret code to open the small door and slip inside, closing it quickly behind her before any of the street humans could notice.

Once inside, she stood with her back against the door, as she always did, reveling in the silence and space not filled with human heat or odor. The door led straight down into what the resistance had taken to calling Alice's rabbit hole, and Typha closed her eyes and took the plunge. She landed with a soft thud on the cushioned pads which were standard equipment below all the rabbit holes, and only then did she open her eyes.

The room she landed in was empty, which wasn't of a surprise. This was a council room and wasn't usually occupied except during important meetings or when all the members of the resistance were present and there was need for more sleeping and living space. Typha hurried through the maze of tunnels leading back into the living quarters of the permanent residents…the same living quarters where she was born and lived until she was sixteen and taken by the elders to work for the government as a scientist.

Aspen looked up as Typha rushed into the living room; his face flashed a warm smile and he reached for her. Once he folded her in his loving arms, stroking her hair, he expressed his worry.

"What's going on, Typha?" he murmured in her ear. "Is something wrong? No one was expecting you tonight."

Usually when an outside member showed up unexpectedly it was bad news. Typha hastened to reassure him.

"Nothing's happened…at least, nothing bad", she murmured, enjoying the embrace.

She forgot why she was there, lost in the warmth of Aspen's love, feeling the heat of his breath on her cheek, and thinking she came down there for a romantic get together. She ran her fingers through his long blond hair. She shook herself and remembered why she ventured out with so little warning.

Typha stirred, awoke, and groaned. She was still on the floor where she collapsed last night. The light streamed into the room, artificial sunlight warning her the hour was getting late. She'd better hurry if she hoped to get to the lab on time. She couldn't be late. In ten years, she'd never been late because to be late is to call attention to yourself, to make the elders wonder what you've been doing with your time.

She rolled over in the small room, bumped her hip against the bed, and groaned again. She was going to have a bruise. She stood, fully dressed in the coat and boots she wore on her escapade last evening. Her blouse and skirt were crumpled from being slept in and her jacket lost a button during the night.

She went to work sewing the button back on. It wasn't like she had a lot of spare clothes. This was her only jacket, and she was required to wear a suit. She pulled her other blouse and skirt out of the chute where she placed them two nights ago for waterless cleaning. They were sharply pressed by the pressure in the chute and she was grateful that in all the excitement she remembered to clean her outfit. Changing out of her rumpled outfit, she placed it into the cleaning chute, from which she'd retrieve it tomorrow morning.

Typha skipped her usual Manna breakfast. She did have her usual sip of water, and thanks to her collapse before bedtime last night she was able to have an extra sip. The water always tasted so good, it was a shame there was so little of it. She always wondered about that, as her great-grandmother's books talked about water as if it were in great abundance.

One time, at work, she found she was temporarily able to access the computer records of the elders through some strange coincidence of matching access codes, and she researched several topics in the few weeks before they changed the access codes. Water was one of them.

She discovered that, in the time before the transformation, water was taken for granted. Although it wasn't equally available everywhere, in most of the United States there was plenty of drinking water and people tended not to think about it much. They bathed in it, they played in it, they sprinkled it on lawns to make grass grow, and they used it without thought to future shortages. It didn't seem conceivable to most of them there could be a shortage of water.

"I had to come, because I had an idea, a spectacular idea, and I needed to share it and perhaps get something going quickly."

Aspen called the local leaders of the resistance together. They sat around the living room, Typha assuring them there was no need for a formal meeting in the council room. With excitement choking her voice, she outlined her idea, gesturing toward the bookshelves lining the large room, filled to overflowing with books they were able to preserve following the transformation.

"We can preserve the greatest ideas in history", Typha enthused. "We can prevent the growing threat of deterioration for all these works, whether sublime or mediocre. It's in our hands, and we never thought of it. I know time seems limited with all the other things we're trying to do to bring the world back from the edge of insanity, but if we do manage, what meaning will it have it all the ideas have become as extinct as all the other species?"

Annapolis, a short, near-sighted young man with thinning hair, nodded enthusiastically as Typha spoke. He grabbed a book off the shelves, and began to read.

"Call me Ishmael."

As he spoke, Sassy wrote down the words on a nearby tablet. He read approximately a page as Sassy wrote. Overcome by his natural shyness, flushed at being the center of attention, he sat triumphantly on the couch and lapsed back into his normal quietness, though now with an air of purpose and determination.

The group burst into confused conversation, everybody speaking at once as they reacted to the novel idea. Drysdale, the unofficial leader of the local group, finally spoke and the group fell silent.

"I think it's a wonderful idea", Drysdale began, "but..."

He paused for effect, looking around the eager group, all sitting forward on the edge of their chairs, ready to jump into action at the first opportunity.

"We might have some problems completing the project because of the limits on paper and ink", he said, with the quiet common sense which contributed greatly to his rise to a position of respect.

Drysdale was in his late 60s and had seen a great many things the rest of them had not yet experienced. Tending toward quiet contemplation, he was usually the one who actually made things happen because he thought through all the necessary steps before he leapt into action. Right now, Typha thought, his careful planning is exactly what we need.

She curbed her impatience at the voice of reason, and reminded herself sometimes a good tug on the reins was exactly what she needed. Typha admired Drysdale immensely; in fact, she adored him as one would adore a father. Typha, unsure of who her father was, built her fantasies around Drysdale, creating elaborate scenarios imagining him as her father. She listened as he spoke, praising her for her idea and outlining the things to consider before they undertook the far-reaching project.

"This will be a bigger job than most of us imagine", he said. "These books took centuries for the writers to write, and they could easily take us centuries to copy. In order to maximize the impact of our project, especially in view of the possibility that we might run out of supplies before we finish, I think we need to begin by making a long-term plan of action. The first thing we need to do is establish a priority list, so those works which are the most important or valuable are preserved first. This won't always be easy. For instance, it's not hard to make a choice between William Shakespeare and Neil Simon...but how do you choose between *Hamlet* and *MacBeth*? Does literature have priority over non-fiction, or vice versa? All these things need to be resolved before we begin; otherwise, we'll just set out willy-nilly and burn ourselves out long before we accomplish anything."

Drysdale was right. Drysdale was usually right. The group went to work setting up a working group to create a list of recommendations for prioritizing the books; the entire group would decide by consensus which works should be preserved first. Drysdale would spread the word throughout the national and international networks, to get an international operation going and maximize the impact of the project.

Typha glowed with pride. Lately she felt like she wasn't much help to the resistance because of her government activities, although they always assured her the things she was doing were most important, especially since the failure of her lab could mean the failure of humankind.

It was late when Typha crept back to her room, but in spite of the hour she was too excited to sleep. She lay in her bed wrapped in the warm glow of accomplishment, a glow she hadn't felt since her mother died and she began working for the elders. She turned over on her stomach and tried hard to get to sleep.

Tomorrow was Sunday and church attendance was mandatory. She couldn't show up with red, tired eyes or yawning like one who'd been out half the night. It wasn't that the elders didn't know she'd been part of the resistance her whole life; it wasn't like they believed she'd given it up when she was given a government job. They only tolerated her non-conformity because she was valuable to them. Sooner or later, someone else would come along who would be able to learn to do the work, in spite of her lackluster training, and then she wouldn't be needed anymore. She frowned as she thought of David...she needed to be more careful.

14

Jason woke early, the smell of bacon and coffee teasing him awake, recalling the years of his childhood. Sunday morning was a time of family activities. Picnics in the park, hikes in the woods, trips to the country to research some wildlife refuge where Mom was surveying the biodiversity, trips to New York City with Dad for a book auction…Sunday had always been Jason's favorite day. Sunday morning had always begun with the smell of bacon and coffee.

Jason slid out of bed, making sure not to wake Kathy. Pulling a thin bathrobe over his pajamas, he headed downstairs to check out the wonderful smells coming from the kitchen. He certainly could do with one of Mom's fluffy omelets this morning.

Entering the kitchen, he was disappointed when he realized Dad was the one standing in front of the stove frying the bacon, but Dad was also a great cook and the scrambled eggs he was whipping up in a large bowl would be welcome. Soon the entire family gathered around the dining room table, Kathy rubbing her eyes sleepily as she tried to join in the rather boisterous family breakfast.

After breakfast, Anna and Kathy sent the men to the park to play an impromptu game of touch football while they cleaned up. After nearly a week, Kathy was beginning to feel at home with her in-laws and she was looking forward to a quiet Sunday. She and Anna made small talk as they washed dishes and swept the floors. They didn't talk about the events of the past few months, or the ways in which all their lives had changed so dramatically.

There were plenty of conversations over the past week and Kathy was beginning to understand how serious everything was. She'd lived her whole life in a world that gave her the freedom to choose her path in life, and she was just beginning to realize her freedom might be threatened by the new order.

Kathy was having trouble understanding how Congress could introduce bills requiring women to have children, requiring them to be removed from the schools. Weren't they protected from discrimination? Anna explained that the new bills Congress was introducing to remove women from the workplace were in line with the way the Supreme Court interpreted the Constitution. The 14th Amendment, which extended rights to all citizens, defined a citizen as male. This view had been upheld by the Supreme Court many times.

Since the Equal Rights Amendment never passed, most of the rights enjoyed by women were given by Congress. Without Constitutional protection, Congress was able to take them away. The Supreme Court was expected to be compliant; they had been overturning precedent right and left on the basis of their own committed religious devotion.

Jason grew so quiet as Anna told them about the policy changes at the university, Kathy was afraid he didn't believe his mother. One glance at the growing anger on his face told her all she needed to know: he did believe it and he felt helpless. They were all afraid, and they were trying not to let each other see they were afraid.

Anna remained busy all week, and hadn't had as much time as she would like to spend with the kids. She prepared resolutions and white papers for the coalition, wrote letters to Senators and Congressmen, and edited a speech she was to deliver at a national gathering of the Faculty Coalition in Seattle next weekend. In addition, she was asked to be editor for an independent newspaper the Coalition created to deal with issues of importance in resisting the transformation.

She modeled the anticipated impacts of accelerated population growth on already stressed ecosystems, and the ability to expand agricultural production to the level necessary to support a rapidly increasing population. She finished writing her article on her results yesterday and posted it to several national publications late yesterday afternoon. Now she felt entitled to a day to just sit back with her feet up and relax with the kids.

Simon got out the Scrabble board and set up for a family game. Anna protested there was too much to be done to play Scrabble, but she allowed herself to be persuaded. For the next couple of hours, the recent difficulties dissolved as they laughed and played and quibbled over whether "typha" would be an accepted word. Anna won three out of four games, in spite of the ultimate rejection of "typha", and she was carried in triumph around the backyard on Jason's broad shoulders. She protested it was too much, but Jason, laughing, insisted on the triumphal parade.

With a knock on the door, the new reality intruded on their peaceful Sunday afternoon. It was Louise from next door. She invited them to join in a neighborhood party...a bonfire celebrating the transformation.

"Be sure to bring all the books that need to be burned", Louise said. "We're going to be getting rid of all the nasty, unpleasant, and immoral filth that's filled the world for so long."

Anna asked her what they were burning.

"Oh, just anything that is wrong or bad", Louise answered vaguely. "You know, stuff that gives people wrong ideas. The president is going to lead it off; he'll be starting the burning at the White House. He'll light the first match himself. It's on TV, you know."

Louise looked suspiciously beyond Anna to the family sitting around the room without the TV.

"Haven't you been watching the President's speech?" she asked accusingly.

"We've been busy today, and we forgot about it", Anna answered. "The kids are in town for a short time and we were doing family things."

"Oh, well, I suppose that's all right, then", Louise sulked. "After all, family is important."

Anna told Louise they'd try to make the bonfire. As soon as the door closed behind the visitor, Simon clicked the knob on the silent TV. The President's speech was over but the political analysts were still discussing it. The president called on everyone in the country to pitch in and purge the nation of "wrong" ideas. Book burnings were urged, along with records, movies, and magazines. He suggested the book burnings should be joyous occasions, family or neighborhood get-togethers, complete with wiener roasts, marshmallows, and sing-alongs to celebrate the cleansing.

The camera cut back to the President. He was going to get the festivities going with a bonfire of his own. He'd collected a handful of books which needed to be destroyed and he would personally light the match to set an example for other citizens to follow.

The president personally selected the titles he was going to burn: *The Population Bomb* by Paul Ehrlich; *The Limits to Growth* by the Club of Rome; *Maybe One* by Bill McKibben; and *An Essay on Population* by Thomas Malthus. All the works warned against the dangers of overpopulation and suggested new, more sensible population policies. The last thing to be added to the fire was the 1973 Report on Population prepared by a White House-appointed commission, which discovered all those years ago that further population growth would not be good for the country and recommended stabilization of the US population. The report was considered too hot to handle and was placed on a shelf and ignored; now it was brought down off the shelf to be destroyed forever.

Anna watched in horror as the President struck the match and lit the small pile of books piled on the White House lawn. Although there were many copies of these books in print, the symbolic gesture set a dangerous precedent. It wasn't just the burning of these particular books; it was the destruction of ideas that was dangerous. Besides, once ideas began to be destroyed, people often weren't far behind.

Anna winced as a bright orange glow leapt up from the yard next door. Simon locked the door. Slowly, wordlessly, he began pulling books out of the bookshelves which lined nearly every wall. Jason brought in boxes from the garage and the four of them piled books into the boxes. They weren't sure where they were going to take them, but they knew they had to put them somewhere out of sight.

15

It was getting harder to concentrate on work. Typha's hands went through the motions of caring for the precious tissue cultures, making sure they had the water and nutrients they needed from the dwindling stores of resources and venting the oxygen into the external world enclosed by the dome. Her movements were flawless even in her distraction, trained by years of skillful practice.

David watched with a painful combination of admiration, respect, and desire. He could tell Typha was distracted but he didn't question her too closely. Making friends with Typha wasn't easy, as he'd discovered. She was cautious, quiet, and shy. She responded to his friendly overtures in a perfunctory manner, never volunteering information about herself or her life.

David was intrigued. She was an exotic woman, a woman of mystery, something rare and refreshing in a world of women who wore their lives on their sleeves, trailing hordes of screaming kids as they moved from church to shops to home, carrying Bibles ostentatiously displayed. Funny, he'd never seen Typha with a Bible, and that funny, non-Biblical name she had…he was sure it must mean something and he had the feeling she was about to tell him its meaning the day he asked, but she checked herself so quickly. Could it be her name meant something forbidden? He tried looking it up in the computer databases available for information gathering purposes but it gave him back an error message indicating there was no such word. Still…

Typha was aware of David watching her, though he seemed to be totally involved in his own work. For the first time, she had an intern for whom she could find some grudging respect. David wasn't an idiot, senses dulled by generations of inbreeding and poor education. His mind was quick and he picked up abstract concepts and physical activities with equal speed. David was going to be a fine botanist.

Typha shivered. The one comfort she had always taken in her position was the knowledge that none of her interns had proven capable of taking over her position; now she had plenty to be worried about. Most of the privileges she enjoyed, such as her room to herself and a certain willingness on the part of the authorities to look the other way when she took an unauthorized walk, were the direct result of her indispensability. As soon as someone, a male from a more acceptable background, could be trained in her job...Typha shuddered, remembering her mother, blood streaming down her cheeks as she turned her face away and died in the interrogation room. Typha knew too much to be simply released from her position and allowed to resume her former life.

She shook off the disturbing thought, along with the knowledge of David watching her, possibly a spy for the elders, and returned to the thoughts which distracted her...the book preservation project in full swing within the deep labyrinthine tunnels of the resistance. She felt honored to have been selected in the first round of voting to help establish priority lists of works to be saved. The group met every evening, though Typha was not able to sneak past the eagle eyes of the army every night and joined them only when she could.

Drysdale and Annapolis were drawing up a plan for the actual preservation project and were in daily consultation with the far-flung leaders of other resistance cells. Word of the project spread throughout the network and they received offers of help, offers of books to be copied, and a myriad of suggestions about which books should be preserved first and the methods they should adopt for the project.

They had already made some modifications to the original plan, moving away from the idea of paper and ink writing and toward the idea of creating the works in a computer database, where they could be accessed and printed should the political and social situation ever permit. Storage would be less of a problem, and if they backed them up in enough places, it would be more difficult to find and destroy all copies. One thing the resistance had in abundance was computer knowledge and computer equipment. Even with the self-imposed limits on network connections because of the ease of tracing internal messages sent by computer, the computing power of the resistance was the most impressive in existence.

The elders couldn't boast of anything to compare. They lacked the knowledge and the creativity to expand computer capabilities and were still using computer programs developed before the transformation. The total distrust of intellectual achievement and higher learning locked them into a stagnation of ideas and technology that would eventually be their undoing, or so the resistance believed.

In contrast, the members of the resistance continued to enhance and upgrade the computer systems they maintained and create new capabilities in technology. The creativity of the resistance, as well as the intellectual knowledge, swamped that of the authorities by several orders of magnitude. Sooner or later, the imbalance would work to the advantage of the resistance. This belief carried the resistance through many bleak days and nights when victory seemed very far away.

"Oh, no!" Typha shouted, racing to David's side and grabbing his hand, jerking it away from the device he was about to adjust. "No, you must never do that! That device..." she trailed off as she saw the look on David's face.

She realized her own face must reflect the terror she felt as she saw her terror reflected in the eyes of her apprentice. More calmly, she continued "that device, you must never adjust that until you've learned all the settings. It's the device which controls the oxygen release into the external dome of the city, and adjusting it improperly could result in a complete shutoff of the oxygen supply worldwide."

Typha was calming down, aware she had narrowly averted disaster, and wanting to explain rationally why she reacted so viscerally. David nodded, his face grave and ashen. Typha realized she had scared him and for the first time, she realized she actually screamed when she saw him reaching toward the dial.

She remembered a saying her granddad used to have, something left over from his childhood, and she giggled and said to David, in a mock-serious voice "No, no, no! Don't touch that dial!" Her characteristic shyness took over, and she looked away in embarrassment at her moment of intimacy.

David watched her in silence for the rest of the day. At first he was scared by her sudden sharp reaction but now he was puzzled. What was the meaning of the giggle, the silly saying? Where did that come from? He'd never heard it but it sounded like it had meaning to her, some meaning she thought he would understand. He felt angry because he couldn't understand, left out of some joke both wonderful and meaningful but which belonged to another place, perhaps even another time, he was totally unfamiliar with.

He wanted to understand. He wanted to giggle with her, to let her know he understood her joke, to feel he was part of her world. He wanted to tell her he loved her and he almost said it. Shaking his head, he returned to his work, careful to touch only those dials that were familiar. Someday, he hoped, he would be able to understand all those things about her that were puzzling, charming, mysterious, and alluring. He craved the opportunity to be part of her world.

That's funny, he thought. I never think about her becoming part of my world. The thought made him frown. He knew, instinctively, Typha was from somewhere else, some background which didn't include elders and scripture and piety worn like a badge. What else didn't it include, he wondered? What *did* it include? He tried to imagine Typha in his world, visiting his home, his parents, his nineteen siblings, and the thought was so unpleasant he almost wanted to cry.

To imagine Typha fitting into such a setting was ....distressing. What was it? What made Typha different? And how was it possible being different could be so appealing in a world where all rewards accrued to being the same? David changed his lab jacket for his outdoor jacket almost in a daze and wandered home along the crowded, narrow street, lost in thoughts he suspected vaguely were somehow subversive.

16

Anna closed her eyes and breathed deeply. The smell of fresh air was rejuvenating and for the first time in days she forgot about the nasty business going on around her. She forgot about the book burnings and she forgot about the arrest of her daughter-in-law. She forgot about the new policies at the school and she forgot about Childcare for Homemakers.

Pulling on her wading boots, she stepped into her wetland, first checking for water moccasins. This was breeding season and she needed to cautious. The snakes were particularly aggressive during breeding season and she wouldn't want to disturb a mating pair. Although water moccasins weren't generally thought to be in Iowa, there had been a few unconfirmed sightings and Anna had seen at least one in this wetland. No sign of snakes, so she proceeded carefully through the wetland, stopping to admire the small stand of cattails still holding its own despite all the difficulties they faced getting this wetland going. In spite of being despised in some circles, many species of cattails were valuable members of a healthy wetland community and Anna was thrilled to see them in her wetland, their fuzzy brown flower heads waving in the gentle breeze.

Anna spoke quietly to the cattails, verbally expressing her approval of their perseverance, and then scolded herself for the silly, unscientific action. Oh, well, it didn't hurt anyone, certainly not the cattails, and it gave her a warm, comfortable feeling. The wetland was a wonderful place to be and Anna was beginning to feel somewhat normal again.

There was a cry behind her. Her students trailed behind, not as used to the steep, marshy path as she was, and she let them take their time. They were adults and they knew the way, so she wasn't worried about them getting lost. They were as committed to saving this system as she was and she wasn't worried they'd behave badly and damage the ecosystem. She went ahead and got to the wetland first. Now they were catching up and shouting out to find out exactly where she was.

Anna gave a quick response so they could determine her position, then turned back toward the wetland, surveying it with the proud eyes of a mother watching her child receive an award for excellence. This was a good wetland and was getting better every day. She set up a wetland mitigation bank at the school over a decade ago, and this wetland was one of the first fruits of the bank.

She was particularly proud of the role the students played in turning the mitigation project into a reality. Without the tireless efforts of a group of dedicated students, she wasn't sure she could have made it happen. The faces of the students changed from semester to semester but their enthusiasm never waned. This was their wetland, and they loved it as much as she did. Even after being reassigned to other professors, they continued to make the weekly journey to monitor the success of the restoration.

Anna, unconcerned about water and mud, sat in the shallows letting the cool water wash over her. Even sitting, it only came up slightly past her waist. She lay back in the soft mud, hands behind her head, cradled by a soft bed of water cress growing near the bank. She stared up at the nearly cloudless sky, just now shedding the soft pink light of the sunrise and ready to burst forth in the full radiance of a sunny day. Anna was content, and enjoyed the feeling of how right the world looked from this vantage point.

Anna was awakened from her reverie by the splash of cold, slimy mud on her cheeks. Jared, one of the graduate students, stood nearby, hands suspiciously muddy, grinning like a naughty little boy caught with his hand in the cookie jar. With a similar grin, she scooped up a handful of soft dark mud, shaped it into a ball, and flung it at him. Her aim was impeccable and the mud caught him mid-chest, the ball flattening into a grimy mess on impact just as Carolyn and Jay came up behind him. The mud ball fight was on.

For about four minutes, the three students and their young-at-heart professor exchanged mud cannons until all four of them were covered with a black sludge which would probably never quite wash out, leaving their field clothes indelibly stained with an eternal reminder of joy and fun. The battle ended nearly as suddenly as it began and they were all declared winners, and losers, equally. Treaties were formalized with friendly, dirty hugs, and the group settled into the work of documenting survival rates from last summer's planting.

The morning's work was satisfying, and the survival rates this year were even better than last year. Anna and Jared packed the water samples they collected into coolers stored in the bed of the battered old pick up they kept for field work, and waved good-bye to the other students as they headed back to the lab to complete the day's work with water quality testing to document the success of their detoxification efforts. Carolyn's specimen samples were also in the coolers, ready for her to begin testing after her afternoon classes. As Jared drove back to the lab, Anna relaxed in the passenger seat and reflected with contentment on the successful restoration of what had once been a filthy, toxic hole in the ground.

When they returned to the school, Anna was jolted back to the unpleasant reality of the past weeks. Jason and Kathy were in the lab, methodically removing books and packing them for storage. They found a temporary storage site, they told her, where the books would be safe for a short time. It would only need to be a short time, Jason assured her, because this madness was surely only going to be temporary. The country was going through some sort of collective mania, and in a few days they would wake up, and the enormity of what happened would hit them. Things would get back to normal and they could resume the lives they were used to.

Anna wished she could believe him; she wished she could believe he believed it, but the hollow emptiness of his eyes belied the forced optimism of his words. Kathy was uncharacteristically silent, her ebullience faded into an almost robotic stupor as she grabbed books one by one off the shelf and stuffed them into a box.

"What about your books, sweetie?" Anna asked Jason. "Have you thought about how you're going to protect your own library?"

"We have friends back home who are on board with the embryonic resistance that's formed on the coast. They're getting our books boxed up, and will store them with their own. They're also packing up our CDs and DVDs."

Anna nodded. She and Jared unpacked the water samples and ran them through a series of chemical analyses. During the periods spent waiting for reactions to occur, they assisted Jason and Kathy with the books. Several other faculty members had also begun packing up their libraries and were interested in finding out what safe place Jason discovered. Jason, not suspicious by nature, was unwilling to tell anyone, even members of the faculty coalition, for fear they would accidentally reveal the location. He did agree to add the other faculty libraries to the already stored books and make sure they stayed safe until the worst was over.

The faculty coalition met later in the afternoon in response to the recent threats from book burning mobs. Things had gotten worse in the past couple of weeks and the coalition no longer met openly; they found a place off campus and developed a network of messengers to keep lines of communication open. All over the country, faculty coalitions were forming and they were all turning their faces toward Ames, where Anna rapidly emerged as a leader and driving force behind what people were beginning to call The Resistance.

That morning Dean Ryan stopped by Anna's office on an unannounced visit. Anna wasn't sure what the visit was about; she was out in the wetland when he arrived, and she had only a rather cryptic note to let her know he had been there.

Harry bustled into her lab shortly after she returned and asked her where she was all morning. Had she been at some sort of meeting? Anna told him no, she hadn't been at a meeting. She'd been out in the wetland bank collecting data. Visibly relieved, Harry hung around for a couple of minutes, engaging in trivial small talk.

Anna had little doubt she was being watched and she reported on the incident to the coalition. After a short discussion, they decided by voice vote to meet only in the evening, at times when none of them would be reasonably expected to be in their office. They forwarded the results of the vote to the other campuses to alert them to the possible danger.

Anna was quiet over dinner. The day was a roller coaster ride, jerking her from a semblance of normality back into the perverseness of the new, sinister world. The delicious stew Kathy made did little to lift her spirits and the light chatter around her served only as a cover for her moodiness.

After dinner they clustered in the living room around the TV for the president's speech. They avoided the speeches most of the time, but Simon insisted it was important to keep track of what was going on. Tonight the president had an important announcement he wanted to make, so precisely at the stroke of 8:00, Simon clicked on the television.

The face of the president filled the screen. Anna felt a strange, creeping sensation start at the base of her spine and move upward. There was something not right in the president's face. His eyes were beginning to look manic, like a man who had taken leave of his sanity. The president was speaking and she forced herself to concentrate on his words.

"This is a glorious day for the country, a blessed day", he was saying. "The doctors have confirmed the blessed news. The first lady is pregnant. She is doing her part for the good of the country, the good of the world, to fill the world with Americans. She has committed her life to fulfilling her proper duty as the wife of a fertile American male."

The camera moved off the president and panned over the first family, lingering on the face of the first lady. Anna gasped and heard the rest of the family gasping with her. The First Lady, always vivacious and energetic, looked like a different person altogether. She looked…exhausted, drained of all her vitality. Even more noticeably, she looked unhappy. Anna couldn't shake off the feeling she was seeing the future written in the dull, sad eyes of the First Lady. The future for fertile women, anyway. And the future didn't look good.

17

Aspen rolled over and leaned on his elbow, watching Typha sleep. He always woke early, even before the light went on in the dome, not that the dome lights could be seen in the underground hideout. He loved looking at Typha when she slept. She seemed so young, so innocent, and so frail when she was asleep, and he felt his protective instinct surge. Once she awoke, the illusion of frailty would disappear and she would be the strong, independent, and educated woman he loved so deeply, but it was sort of nice from time to time to see the delicate frailty he knew was always just underneath the surface.

He was painfully aware of the deep sorrow Typha still carried within her. He was the first person to meet her when she returned to the resistance following her mother's death. He held her close, grieving with her as she wept uncontrollably. She told him, in broken sobs, the experience of watching her mother's interrogation, the hours and days of brutal torture, the strength and endurance her mother exhibited to the end.

When the tears turned to anger, he sat in compassionate silence as she vented her rage. When the anger yielded to despair and depression, he held her for long hours as she rocked and cried; he stroked her hair and held her tight in his strong arms. He confessed his love for her, and one glorious night, he demonstrated his love physically.

Now he was pensive. Things were increasingly difficult lately, and several members of the resistance had been rounded up and interrogated. The group's living quarters were decked in black almost continuously and Aspen feared for Typha. He listened as she described the new lab assistant, this young intern who was so competent, so capable, so eager to learn, and he heard the undertone of fear in her voice.

Aspen understood what Typha feared. He knew her safety relied on her continued importance to the elders and the new intern was a threat to her safety. It frightened him to think of his Typha in the hands of the interrogators.

Last week Aspen took a foolish risk and snuck out to get a look at the new intern, the young man known to him only as King David. He went to the lab and waited for the end of the shift. When David came out of the building, he nearly wept. This was a young man to be afraid of in more ways than one. He was handsome and strong, and Aspen could tell by the way he watched Typha as she left that he was in love with her. Aspen trusted Typha but he didn't trust David. He followed him home.

David lived in one of the better sections of the city, an area where a family might actually have four rooms. The apartment he lived in was several stories up, but it was roomier than most of the others, suggesting David's family had some importance to the elders.

Aspen watched for several minutes. He learned David was one of twenty children, and his mother still showed signs of the pretty young woman she had been before childbearing and the stresses of raising a large family broke her down and turned her into a defeated, tired looking woman, old before her time.

David apparently was not yet married, which was unusual for a man of his age and position. Although Aspen wasn't sure exactly how old he was, he appeared to be about Typha's age, and usually a man his age would have been married off long enough ago to have fathered at least five children. Aspen puzzled over that for some time. Was David an undesirable? It didn't seem likely, given his position and the apparently high social status of his parents.

Aspen was nearly captured on that trip, and Drysdale took him to task quite sternly. He hadn't tried to leave the hideout since, but he was so concerned about Typha it nearly destroyed him when she didn't show up for several days. Just as he was getting so desperate he was going to take a risk again, she showed up this evening. She was being followed, she reported, and hadn't been able to get away to attend any of the meetings of the book preservation group for fear of giving away their location.

Tonight the guards were diverted by another subversive somewhere across the city, a poorly trained subversive who wasn't part of the resistance and would now be turned over to the interrogators for his trouble. Typha was able to slip away for a visit. Everyone was happy to see her, and she joined in a short memorial service for the members who'd been captured that week.

She spent the night at the hideaway, much to Aspen's delight, and they explored the erotic dimensions of their relationship with unparalleled excitement. After a particularly energetic session of lovemaking, they collapsed, exhausted, to sleep in each other's arms.

Now Aspen rolled on his back, hands clasped behind his head, and breathed a sigh of contentment. For just this brief time, it was possible to put the past out of his mind and think only about the present. This was the impact Typha had on him, making him feel life was good and about to get better, as she wrapped him in the warmth of her love. In time, Aspen told himself, they would get married, and have children...he paused, a sour note creeping into the reverie.

Typha didn't want to have children. She was worried about the bloated population which had already drained most of the planet's resources and didn't feel it was a good idea to continue the reproductive madness. Aspen frowned, biting his lip. Perhaps, he thought, perhaps....just one.

Typha stirred beside him, stretching in delicious contentment in the morning air. Wrapping her arms around Aspen, she allowed herself a respite from the worries that were so prevalent of late. She allowed herself to relax in Aspen's embrace as he murmured sweet, soft endearments in her ear. In minutes, they were once again making love, not in the energetic desperation of the night before, but slowly, leisurely, lingering over every touch, every kiss.

After a raucous breakfast with the gang, the jokes flying about the nasty, mineral-based "manna", Typha knew it was time for her to depart. The longer she remained underground, the more likely it was her absence would be noted and the guards would be on the lookout for her. She slipped out through a remote rabbit hole as far from the center as she could manage and still get back to her room without being noticed. There was no sign of the guards as she emerged.

The dome was just beginning to be light; since it was Saturday, they left the lights off later. Workers were allowed to come to work an hour later on Saturday and most chose to use the hour to gain a little additional sleep. The lights were still in the slight dimness that preceded the full, blazing daytime light which signaled the beginning of an active day.

Typha looked up at the light source and remembered some of the things she read from a past when the world was on natural light. Before the transformation countries were in different time zones because of the rotation of the Earth. Large countries, like the US, were divided into different time zones, with the day getting earlier as you moved west across the continent. In the interest of synchronizing business and worship activities, the daylight hours were adjusted to one single time zone for the whole world after the dome was built. It was also easier than trying to simulate the natural time zones, and since it was easier, it could be done at less cost.

Typha wished she had seen the sun at least once. It must have been something indeed, since so many ancient people worshipped it as a god.

With the daylight creeping through the city, Typha realized she didn't have time to go home before she headed to the lab. She allowed herself to remain longer with Aspen than was prudent.

Scowling as she picked her way through the waking masses of the currently homeless, she scolded herself about the risks she was taking lately. And it wasn't just her. Drysdale pulled her aside last night to tell her Aspen ventured out a week ago to check on her. The entire resistance was restless, and Drysdale was worried that a foolish recklessness was one of the reasons for the recent spate of captures. People were getting careless and taking unnecessary risks. Something needed to happen soon or lack of caution would jeopardize the entire resistance.

Work was quiet all day. David was uncharacteristically silent and reserved so Typha had plenty of time to think as she went about her duties. She agreed with Drysdale. Something needed to happen to restore the morale of the resistance, relax the tension everyone was feeling, and relieve the exhaustion. Tiredness was the greatest enemy of caution, and everyone needed a rest. Typha had a nagging feeling at the back of her mind things were about to heat up again and they would need all the energy they could get.

18

Anna closed and locked the door of the classroom. Teaching grew more difficult by the day. Her class now was totally male, as females were refused entrance to the science program. Many of the males, especially undergraduates who were not science majors, developed a superior attitude, believing there was nothing they could learn from a female and they were only serving their time in an outdated classroom with a female teacher who was a holdover from a more chaotic time, a time where the natural order of things disappeared and the world turned upside down. The classroom was more like a battlefield than a place of learning.

Anna was lost in thought as she walked across the quad to her office. She'd been moved out of her office in the science building and given a smaller office in the Center for Professional Homemakers. She barely managed to keep her classroom and she fought a long and bitter fight to maintain her lab space, an arrangement she realized was only temporary. If it weren't for the efforts of Jared and Jay, she might be out on the street by now.

Carolyn graduated just before the school implemented a new policy which said no more female students would be grandfathered. She and Anna rushed madly to make sure she could get her dissertation written and defended because they were aware the change was in the works. Now Carolyn, a fully trained Ph.D., discovered there were no jobs that would accept her. She fell into a deep depression and Anna was worried about her.

Anna turned the key and gasped in horror. Someone had searched her office. Everything was in disarray, her empty bookshelves overturned and her papers no longer neatly filed but instead scattered all over the small room. Whoever did this also let her parrot out of the cage and poor Polly was flying around the office, desperately trying to understand what was happening to her. The birdcage had been stomped on and lay on the floor, flattened and unusable. Polly's food and water dish were emptied maliciously over a pile of graded student papers which were ready to be returned. Anna sank down in the middle of the pile of scattered paperwork and cried.

She only cried for a minute. Straightening her back and shoulders with resolve, she stopped being depressed and let anger wash over her. Depression, she reasoned, would sap her strength. Anger would give her the motivation she needed to keep going, to make the best of a horrifying situation. Anna had never been the sort of woman to give into depression when things got tough and she wasn't going to take the easy way out now.

She reached for the camera hanging on a hook just outside her office and documented the vandalism. She snapped picture after picture, from every possible angle. She downloaded the pictures onto her computer, e-mailed them on her private account to all the members of the faculty coalition, and sent them to the other member campuses throughout the world. This was a call for action, and Anna would not be disappointed.

Within minutes, e-mails poured in from all over the world, expressing support, anger, determination, or simply shock. The international network mobilized immediately. Anna felt a ray of hope as she realized the power they had harnessed. The network was connected.

By the end of the day, a database was created with the purpose of documenting any and all incidents of vandalism, harassment, or terrorism perpetrated not just against members of the coalition, but against anyone. Members were held responsible for making sure incidents were reported promptly and each region created a rapid response team locally to deal with sudden events and take the necessary counteractions immediately. Although the central command of the response team would be out of Ames, Anna was relieved that there were a couple of other leaders beginning to step forward. Anna accepted an offer from members in Fargo, North Dakota, to take on management of the database and help coordinate efforts to take a little of the workload off her slender shoulders.

Other members around the country offered their skills and time, and people who previously hesitated to do more than lurk in the shadows began to come forward and join the resistance fully. Anna found out later the decisive moment for many of them was seeing the picture of poor Polly, wings flapping wildly in panic, unable to find an island of calm in her newly topsy-turvy world.

As Anna related the experiences over dinner, Kathy was unable to keep silent anymore. She burst out in anger and fear, "What the hell is the matter with them? How could students treat you with so much contempt? Are they so superior at the age of eighteen they can't learn anything from a skilled professional with years of experience, just because she doesn't have a Y chromosome? Why would they be this way? They weren't raised in a world like this. How could they have so quickly adopted such an attitude?"

Eyes blazing, Kathy was just getting started. Jason watched her with alarm, unused to this sort of outburst from his usually calm and collected wife. Simon put his hand on her arm, which had a miraculous calming effect. She looked at him apologetically and shrugged. Her outburst apparently was as unexpected to her as it was to the rest of the family.

Anna was quiet for the rest of dinner. Kathy's outburst echoed her emotions. It was astounding to her the ease with which most of the male students at the university moved into their new roles and abandoned all the ideas and attitudes they learned throughout their life. Anna speculated that perhaps it was easy for most people to move into an attitude of superiority when they were given the chance. She recalled some research done at Stanford, research describing the ease with which ordinary individuals abandoned their principles when given a position of power over others. She decided to look it up first thing in the morning.

The female students, on the other hand, hadn't moved into their new roles nearly so easily. The new program for women students was full of resentful, angry women who lashed out at each other with the slightest provocation. Women who had been at the university for a while and progressed part way through their chosen field of study walked around the building like zombies, with dead eyes and slumped shoulders. They missed classes frequently and often showed up with unwashed, dull hair and disheveled clothes, smelling of alcohol. Anna was concerned many of them wouldn't make it and would end up dropping out before the end of the semester.

While they were at dinner, the phone rang. It was Carolyn, desperate, crying. She wasn't able to deal with her depression, she couldn't keep going like this. All her life she wanted nothing more than to be a scientist, and she was a good one. With her research behind her, a Ph.D. completed, she just received notification from the scientific journal to which she submitted her paper informing her they were no longer allowed to accept papers written by women.

As if such an insult wasn't enough, the editor, in what was probably meant to be a kindly letter, suggested perhaps she might consider getting married. Then if her husband wanted to submit her research under his name, they would be able to reconsider their rejection. Carolyn was crushed. After all her work, it appeared she was destined to be buried alive in a kitchen, bearing children one after another until she was too exhausted to bear any more.

Could Anna come over? Anna agreed and grabbed her coat. Simon and Jason insisted on going with her. Kathy decided it was more than she could handle and shooed them out the door. She'd stay behind, she said in a voice dripping with irony, and clean up the kitchen.

Carolyn didn't answer Anna's knock. With mounting fear, Simon went down to the office and talked to the manager. Could he let them into the apartment? The manager was unwilling to violate the privacy of a tenant by opening the door. Simon decided to take advantage of the new situation in the country, and explained he was worried about the ability of a female to take care of herself properly. As one of her closest male friends, he was hoping to take responsibility for her so she could be properly protected. The manager, nodding with understanding, handed Simon a master key. Simon, fear overcoming his feeling of guilt, rushed upstairs where Anna and Jason were trying to get Carolyn to answer the door. He could tell Anna was desperate. Jason was trying, without conviction, to persuade her Carolyn was just in the bathtub and couldn't hear the knock.

Simon turned the master key and swung open the door. He slammed it shut again before Anna had a chance to get into the room. Yelling to Jason to call 911, he raced to where Carolyn was hanging and cut her down. She was still breathing, and Simon began emergency resuscitation measures. Anna pounded on the locked door, yelling at him to let her in. Simon ignored her. Anna couldn't see this.

The ambulance arrived quickly, but it was too late. As they rushed in the door with a stretcher, Anna crowding anxiously in behind them, Carolyn breathed her last. The ambulance attendants worked heroically to try and resuscitate her, but without success. Anna collapsed on the floor, sobbing uncontrollably. Jason crouched beside her, trying to comfort her. Once the ambulance carted Carolyn away, Simon rushed Anna and Jason out of the apartment. They returned home in subdued silence, tragedy draped over them like a shroud.

19

Typha worried about the cultures. Yesterday morning she saw the first sign of blight on the leaves of one of the older plants. She disposed of it quickly, uprooting it and throwing it in the incinerator along with the media where it was growing. Today she saw more spots on other plants. Most of the problem seemed to be restricted to one species, at least for now, but Typha was aware how quickly a disease could evolve and move to other species.

She wrote up a report for the elders, recommending immediate action to stave off problems. She quarantined the infected plants and cleaned the area thoroughly, hoping to stop the disease in its tracks. David was working in a different part of the compound today, learning another aspect of running the lab.

Typha's name on the intercom summoned her into the presence of the council of elders. Wiping her hands, she hurried outside and across the compound to the ornately designed building which housed the council. This facility was the only spot in the city where it was possible to move quickly without stepping on overflowing humanity; the population was diligently prevented from entering the central control zone where the elders spent their time.

Typha had a suspicion the elders deliberately avoided seeing the fruits of their policies. They had no desire to come face to face with the realities of a finite earth and the wall-to-wall overcrowding which overwhelmed the capacity of the earth's resources. They were able to remain isolated from the consequences of their own actions.

Typha was whisked into the inner sanctum where the elders assembled in an emergency meeting. Her report was on the table in front of Elder Samuel, the senior member of the council. He frowned as he leafed through the neatly typed pages.

"What exactly is this about, Typha?" Elder Daniel demanded. "What is the meaning of this report?"

Typha bowed respectfully and advanced to the spot Elder Daniel waved her toward.

"It's pretty self-explanatory, Elder Daniel", Typha said with a deference which never went below the surface. "One of the species of plants has gotten some sort of disease and I've requested guidance from the learned council. I've isolated the diseased plants, and I've thoroughly cleaned the culture chambers to try to prevent any further spread."

Typha stood at attention, stifling any sign of the disrespect she felt for this group. Elder Samuel finished reading the report and slammed it on the table so hard the water glasses shook. His brows knit in a scowl so fierce they would have cowed nearly anyone else, but Typha remembered her mother in the interrogation chamber and stood her ground firmly, refusing to let them see any fear.

"What is this nonsense?" Elder Samuel growled, the anger in his voice barely controlled. "What is this crap?" He pounded the table in front of him for emphasis. "In this report, you inform us that only one species of plant is infected and yet you express the need to do something quickly before other species become susceptible. You write that you worry the disease will adapt quickly! Are you saying you think the disease might *evolve*?!? You know that's impossible!"

Typha held her ground. She'd managed to get this far in life without having mentioned the forbidden word, evolution, but this situation was too grave to stand on ceremony. The elders couldn't wish evolution away just by legislating against it and while she had little use for the elders, she couldn't let the general distaste for science create a disaster of epidemic proportions.

"Sir, those plants are the basis of our society. If anything happens to them, we will no longer be able to maintain life. It's very important we consider all possibilities in devising a plan for dealing with this new contingency."

Typha bowed again, as though to take the sting out of her words.

"If there is any possibility of spread between species, we need to be alert to it."

The elders all frowned at Typha, taking their cue from Elder Samuel, who looked practically murderous. Typha knew she was walking on thin ice, but she also knew all of them relied on the continued health of the plant cultures. She remained silent, not cowering in the face of disapproval, looking calmly back at her accusers. One by one they looked away, unable to hold her gaze.

"I suppose it's possible there might be some other species that were created with susceptibility to the disease", Elder Samuel was saying, "so we probably should take precautions against spread. What do you recommend?"

"I've already isolated the plant species that is infected", Typha began, "and I'd like permission to do a series of cultures on the disease organism in a sterile setting, to see if there is any antibacterial which will kill it. I'd also like…" Typha spoke quietly for about 30 minutes, outlining what she felt was the appropriate plan of action.

Elder Samuel found a way to move toward protecting the plants while avoiding acknowledgement of evolution, and Typha avoided any mention of adaptations or evolution in her short presentation. The council listened intently as she spoke, nodding occasionally to indicate they understood, though always at the wrong place. They were as clueless about science as they were about life outside the walls of this compound.

Most of the elders listened quietly, with only desultory questions designed to point out that they were in charge. After about an hour they dismissed Typha, giving her permission to implement the plan she outlined. She slipped out with relief and returned to the lab. David returned while she was gone, and he stared with horror at the yellow blotches on the leaves of the isolated tissue cultures.

"What's wrong?" he asked, pointing to the isolation chamber.

Typha gave him a brief explanation. She sat him down with the report she'd prepared and the plan she outlined for the elders, so he could familiarize himself with the procedure they were about to set up. Quickly and efficiently, she set up a sterile unit in an unused area of the lab building. She wouldn't be able to move all the plants into the room, though, until she brought maintenance in to prepare the ceiling with the apparatus which breached the dome and allowed the sun's light into the plant chambers. This was essential over the long term, but for now she could keep a few plants alive using artificial light. She chose sample cultures of varying ages and species and arranged them in the sterile room under the light to allow them to get used to the new setting before she introduced the blight.

David looked up from the report, a worried look on his face. He didn't like the sound of what was happening. And he didn't understand some of the references in the report.

"What's this?" he asked Typha as she came out of the sterile room into the main lab. "What do you mean when you say the disease may adapt and spread to other species? I don't understand."

David never heard of evolution, which didn't surprise Typha, since it was a forbidden subject. She patiently began to explain it to him, using the same language Elder Samuel used, that some other species might be susceptible. She told him she was going to be testing the various species to see what sort of future problems they might encounter, and also to see if there was anything which could kill the disease. David nodded slowly. He would do whatever she told him she needed.

In the evening, after lights out, Typha slipped out of her apartment and headed to the closest safe rabbit hole. She needed to do some reading on plant pathogens and evolution in order to prepare her for this new situation. She read these topics when her mother taught her about Botany, but she needed a refresher. Slipping into the reading room, Typha settled in for a long, sleepless night with her books.

20

Anna frowned. The man on the front porch shifted slightly, uncomfortable under her penetrating gaze. Evidently she wasn't going to cooperate and he was tired of having to get rough. It didn't seem worth it to him, but he had his orders.

"Come on, lady", he whined. "Let me come in and look around. I won't disturb anything but what I came for."

To his surprise, Anna smiled, opened the door, and let him enter.

"Come in, officer", she said with feigned warmth. "Come in and look around. I don't want to stand in the way of the law."

Anna was confident. They'd been careful to remove all forbidden books from the house, and all that was left were a handful of innocuous women's magazines and three Bibles. The rest were safely stashed somewhere. Anna didn't even know where Jason put them; they'd needed to move them out of the original storage site once Congress passed the law making certain books illegal.

Joe entered the house cautiously. He had a list of houses which were suspected of having forbidden books and this was one of the highest on the list. He'd been warned he would likely face trouble from these college professor sorts, who weren't giving up their books willingly. Anna didn't look dangerous, especially this morning in her soft bathrobe, but you never could be sure. Joe learned long ago to be cautious no matter who you were dealing with. Too many of his fellow police officers lost their life by letting their guard down against people who looked safe.

Joe stood in the middle of the living room looking around. There were bookcases, all right, lots of them, but they were mostly empty. He saw a book on the end table and picked it up gingerly. It was black leather, with gold embossed words on the cover. It was a bible, and he set it reverently back down on the table. Other than that, all he saw were a few magazines, mostly cooking magazines. He frowned.

"Where are your books?" he asked, jerking his thumb toward the empty bookcases. "Those surely ain't for decoration. They ain't very pretty."

"We got rid of all the books when the law was passed outlawing them." Anna smiled sweetly. She knew he would demand she prove it but she was prepared.

"Oh, really?" Joe growled.

He didn't believe her. These college types didn't usually give up their books so easily. He was really rather sympathetic with them. He didn't see what harm a few books could do, and he thought they should be allowed to keep their books. But he had a job to do. After all, there was a law.

"Where'd you put 'em?"

"Follow me." Anna led him into the backyard to a burn barrel. They prepared this spot last week so they would have some evidence of book destruction to stop questions. "We burned them. Out here."

Joe bent over the burn barrel and stirred the cold ashes. The ashes contained several fragments of books, including a couple of nearly intact spines. He plucked one out of the barrel and squinted at the writing to identify the book.

"On the Origin of Species - Charles Darwin", he read aloud.

This book was at the top of the list of banned books. Pulling another fragment out of the barrel, he read the title.

"Why I'm not a Christian – Bertrand Russell". He frowned. "Not a Christian? Why would anyone not be a Christian?"

He looked closely at Anna's face but she just smiled sweetly, shook her head, and shrugged her shoulders. Plainly she couldn't understand it either. Joe dropped the spines back into the burn barrel and headed back toward the house. Things looked all right, but just to be safe...he'd better search the whole house.

Anna led Joe from room to room, allowing him to search closets and cupboards and under beds. Nothing suspicious turned up, much to his relief. He liked this woman. It was hard to imagine the government could consider her dangerous. She was sweet, and...well, pretty.

Charmed, Joe allowed her to make him a cup of tea and accepted a cookie she offered him. When he left, he was satisfied this was a house fully prepared to follow the law, even a totally ridiculous law. These were good people, Joe thought as he headed down the sidewalk. Good people who know, even when a law doesn't make sense, it's still the law and you have to follow it. And, Joe told himself, I still have to enforce it, even if I don't understand it.

Anna breathed as Joe drove away. She was glad she was alone when he came. She wasn't sure Jason or Kathy could have pulled it off, and she knew Simon would have difficulty. He'd already faced them at the bookstore, where he carefully demonstrated how he destroyed all his original stock and now carried only approved works, such as the writings of Augustine of Hippo and St. Francis. He proudly showed the officer an entire bookshelf of original, signed copies of the Left Behind series and a first edition signed copy of C. S. Lewis's "Surprised by Joy".

When he told Anna about it later, the anger and fear showed in his face. He nearly exploded, he said. He wanted to tell them just where to get off and just how much respect he felt for their asinine, medieval laws. Anna was sure he wouldn't be able to carry it off again.

Jason popped his head in the back door. "Is he gone?"

Anna nodded and Jason entered cautiously, closing the door quietly behind him as though trying to prevent anyone from knowing he was there.

"I saw the patrol car out front and I drove around the block. I wanted to be here to help you, but I thought you would probably handle it better than I would, and I didn't want to accidentally say the wrong thing", he explained.

Anna told him how it went and he fairly whooped because it worked so well. Jason and Kathy were hard at work all morning moving the books from the most recent hiding place. They saw evidence someone had been snooping around. Now they were in serious difficulty.

"I think we're going to have to begin moving them underground", he said. "The underground storage is nearly ready, but I was hoping we could wait a little longer. I've been working on a plan to get it finished and furnished, just in case the resistance needs to go into hiding."

Anna understood. It was possible they would have to take more drastic action. She shivered. Although the sun was shining and it was a beautiful summer day, she felt cold.

21

Typha looked up from her cultures. David slipped into the room behind her and waited for her to finish logging the data. So far things looked good. There was no evidence of susceptibility in any other species, and no sign the pathogen was evolving. It looked as though they were going to be able to isolate the disease and prevent catastrophe. She wiped her hands on a clean towel and looked inquiringly at David. He didn't interrupt her in the lab unless it was important.

"There are some gentlemen out here to see you."

There was a curious, enigmatic look in his eyes and he was strangely subdued. Typha indicated she'd be out in a minute. David slipped back out the door.

Typha sat quiet on her stool, collecting her thoughts. For the past three weeks, she'd been working nearly non-stop, doing everything she could to contain the bacteria before it spread too far. David stayed much of the time, too, but she made him go home at night even if she stayed. It wouldn't do for both of them to be exhausted. She was looking forward to taking a little breather.

She hadn't seen much of Aspen lately with her hectic schedule, and she hadn't had any chance to work on the book preservation project even though it meant so much to her. It would be good to get back to normal.

Typha straightened her shoulders and went out to see who needed to see her. Very curious, she thought. Nobody ever came here. She got the feeling the lab disturbed the complacency of the elders, and they didn't want anyone else to know how things were run. They told the citizens they solved the oxygen problem through prayer, and the citizens, numbed into submission by decades of obedience, believed them. This control center where plant cultures were so carefully nurtured to provide the oxygen scientifically could lead to a loss of credibility for the elders, which would never be tolerated.

What a mess the world had become. How much she longed for the world her grandmother and others so carefully documented and preserved in the photographs and paragraphs of the library she inherited.

The men waiting for her were guards. They came to collect Typha for her appointment with the elders. Typha didn't ask any questions. This was the normal way someone was informed of an appointment with the elders. She itched to pull out her Oxford English Dictionary and read them the definition of "appointment" but she realized the fallout wouldn't be worth the satisfaction she'd get from seeing their surprised faces.

She took off her lab coat and left with the guards, instructing David to be sure and vent the oxygen properly for the night before he closed up. He nodded, a peculiar look on his face, and turned back to his work without speaking a word.

Typha stood before the elders in resignation and despair. She had worried about this day; now she just needed to get through it without letting them see her break. She was officially removed from her post. David, they said, knew the job well, and they had confidence in his ability to run the lab. She wasn't needed any more and she was a known troublemaker. Not to mention, it didn't look right having a woman in such a job. Women were supposed to get married and have children. Not, they hastened to add, that they were suggesting she would be getting married. As an undesirable she wouldn't be allowed to have children, so there was no point in marrying her off.

"For ten years, we've had to keep you in an entire apartment by yourself because we couldn't take the risk of having anyone else room with you. You aren't safe", Elder Samuel was saying. "This has been a tremendous inconvenience and cost for us, and we need the space. So we've cleared out your apartment and moved in a couple with nine children who need and deserve the space."

Typha was numb. She suspected what was coming next. She knew there was little likelihood they were simply moving her to smaller quarters. She wondered if they discovered her secrets in her room: the small supply of candles and the copy of *Bleak House* she was reading and which was stored inside her mattress. If so, they didn't mention it.

Typha was handed over to the interrogators. Her worst fears had come true. No one in her experience ever managed to escape the interrogators and no one ever, to her knowledge, lived through interrogation. The best she could hope for was to remain strong and not give them any information to incriminate the resistance.

Usually a member of the resistance who was outside in danger of being captured would have a vial of poison secreted on their person and it was unusual for a member to fail to use it. The techniques of the interrogators held more fear than death, and members of the resistance went quickly and peacefully to their death to avoid the possibility of breaking in a moment of intense pain. Unfortunately, Typha didn't have a vial because she had been outside for so long she'd grown careless.

The interrogators held both sides of Typha as she was led out of the chamber and down into the labyrinthine maze of the interrogation center. This was familiar territory; she walked those same corridors a decade ago with her mother. On that trip she believed things would work out, her mother would escape, and everything would be all right.

Even as she picked her way through the dark maze, the teenager imagined a daring rescue, Drysdale rushing to save them at the last minute, just like she read in some of her story books when she was a child. Or Mom, brave and fearless, whipping out a knife secreted in her sock (no, it would have to be somewhere else – they'd been searched carefully), and fighting her way valiantly out of the center, mowing down guard after guard as she and Typha fled back into the comforting secrecy of the night.

Typha created many scenarios on the seemingly endless journey through numerous twisting hallways and seemingly infinite doors silently sliding open on their approach, and closing just as silently behind them. With each door and each turn, Typha's spirits dropped lower and lower. She knew each obstacle they passed made the odds of escape more remote. The escape never happened. Mom died at the hands of the interrogators.

They reached the final destination and the forward motion stopped. Typha jerked back to the present, the teenager again merely part of her past. This wasn't Mom's life anymore, she told herself grimly. Now it was her life, and she needed to steel herself for the hell she was about to encounter. She must not risk everything Mom died to protect. She held herself tall and proud, defiantly refusing to show the slightest trace of fear as they strapped her into the interrogation chair.

22

Fires burned everywhere Anna looked. She ran as fast as her legs would carry her, but it was difficult in her bare feet. The gravel road cut her feet to ribbons and the road was covered with bloody footprints marking where she traveled. Anna wished she had time to stop and hide her footprints, fearing someone would be able to trace her by the bloody path she left behind, but knowing she couldn't stop. She had to keep on running....running...running....

"Anna!" She heard Simon beside her, calling her name. He was running, too, so strong, so fit, and she reached out her hand to take his. "Anna! Wake up! You're having a nightmare again."

Simon was shaking her. Anna roused herself with difficulty, the fires fading, the bloody footprints disappearing into the mists of the sleep she left behind. Simon watched her, worried. She realized she must have been screaming or moaning. She wrapped her arms around Simon and held tight.

"Don't ever let go of me", she whispered. "Don't let go of me...I'm afraid of what will happen if you let go of me."

"I won't let go of you, sweetheart", Simon promised with a catch in his voice.

He held her in a tight embrace and stroked her hair. They stayed in the embrace, unable to move apart. The clock ticked loudly on the night table and Simon looked over.

"2:00", he announced. "It's tomorrow. Happy birthday, darling", he said, with a slight, humorless chuckle in his voice.

"Birthday?"

Anna was still dazed. As the mists of the dream faded around her, she remembered. Today was her birthday. She was 52, and they had planned a big party. Jason and Kathy were here from San Francisco, where they were wrapping up final touches on their latest project, an underground film about the resistance which would be broadcast over encrypted channels to all the members for use as an educational tool and recruiting film. Kathy was shooting archival footage to document the daily changes in the world around them. As a birthday treat, they were going to preview them for Anna and Simon.

Anna settled into the soft pillows and tried to get back to sleep. Two hours wasn't enough sleep, not when there was so much to do every day. She hadn't been sleeping well lately, partially because of the frequent nightmares, but she was determined to try.

"Why don't you take some of those pills the doctor gave you, Anna?" Simon was urging her. "You really need to get some sleep."

Anna demurred. "I don't think so tonight. I'm afraid the sleeping pills would just make the nightmares worse."

That was her excuse and she was trying her best to sound adamant. In truth, she was afraid to take the sleeping pills. Though she needed sleep, she was afraid if she took the pills she might not be able to wake up quickly if necessary.

Anna drifted off to sleep and slept without dreaming for the rest of the night. Waking late, she was drawn to the kitchen by the tempting aroma of fresh coffee. The whole family was waiting for her. They had prepared some sort of surprise but they were determined to let her sleep. Now they crowded around her, greeting her warmly, offering her eggs and sausage, filling her coffee cup, and in general making an uncharacteristic fuss over her. She decided not to protest and just sat basked in their love. She ate slowly, savoring every delicious bite. Jason made the breakfast and she was proud to realize he was a good cook.

When they felt they couldn't contain themselves anymore, she was finished. As she started to clear away her dishes and take them into the kitchen, Jason took the plates out of her hands.

"Leave them for now", he said firmly. "They can wait."

He led her into the living room where Simon and Kathy waited impatiently. She settled on the couch beside Simon, nestled as close to him as possible. Jason perched on the arm of the chair where Kathy was seated, and they all watched her with an air of excitement she hadn't seen in a long time.

"Mom", Kathy began. "I have some news for you."

Anna steeled herself. Lately any sentence beginning with those words had not been good.

"Mom, I'm pregnant."

Kathy fairly glowed with pleasure. Anna wasn't sure how to react because she wasn't sure she heard correctly.

"Mom?" Jason peered anxiously into her face. "Mom, are you all right? We hoped it was happy news."

Anna shook herself. She had heard correctly. "I'm fine, Jason. I'm great!"

She grabbed Kathy and wrapped her in a big, warm embrace.

"It just caught me off guard, that's all", Anna said. "I was all steeled for some horrible news."

"It's the only one we plan to have", Kathy said anxiously.

She knew the concerns Anna harbored over the recent turn of events which were already leading to a population explosion. Over the past several months the birth rate nearly tripled and early reports suggested it was probably going to triple again in the next three months. Kathy didn't want to be part of this craziness but she and Jason always planned on having just one child.

They discussed it carefully before deciding to go ahead with their plans, and they worried about what sort of a world they were bringing a child into. One of the things that convinced them was when Simon, in his quiet way, told them he felt with the strangeness in the world, there needed to be some island of normality where people who hadn't embraced the madness could find their space. It wasn't a good time, he said, for the best educated and most skilled people to reject childbirth totally just because everyone else was having so many. Kathy wasn't sure she believed the argument but she found it comforting. Now she anxiously watched Anna, hoping she, too, would see it that way and wouldn't disapprove.

Anna couldn't disapprove. She didn't think it would be right for the reckless decisions of so many foolish people to be the sole deciding factor in such a momentous decision. Jason and Kathy would be wonderful parents. Why shouldn't they have just one child, just because so many people out there were throwing caution to the winds? She let out a whoop of happiness to let them know she was excited. They all settled in to discuss baby names, a breath of fresh air bringing a trace of normality into an increasingly surreal world.

Anna decided not to go to her wetland. After all, it was her birthday and though she usually couldn't think of many other places she'd rather be, she wanted to spend this day with her family. They piled into the little Toyota and went for a drive in the country. When she and Simon were first married, these drives were one of their favorite activities. They continued it throughout their years together, though less often now because of their concern for the deepening environmental problems and their desire not to burn more fuel than necessary. Today was the first drive they'd taken since the transformation began.

Anna watched the countryside fly past her window. Although there weren't yet any major changes evident in the system, she knew the current birth rate couldn't be maintained without having a negative impact on the countryside. As more babies were born, people would seek bigger and bigger houses. As the babies began to grow up and start families of their own, more and more houses would be needed. More food would be required. Plowing and paving of the few remaining natural systems was inevitable in such a population press, and Anna worried about the future.

First you plow the natural areas to feed the growing population; then you pave the plowed fields to find places to put all the new people. Then you don't have enough fields to feed them. More ecosystems would disappear; more species would go extinct. Anna knew Iowa had already lost more than 90% of its natural ecosystems, even without the current population explosion. As corn fields passed by her window, she fell into silent reflection, wondering just where this was going to lead. What sort of a world were they going to leave for the grandbaby? She was silent the rest of the way home but her silence for once wasn't noticed; the exuberant conversation masked her brooding and she was free to explore her own thoughts.

Kathy insisted on clearing the table after dinner. She told Anna she should be allowed to take an evening off for her birthday, and shooed her and Simon into the living room where Jason was busy setting up the DVD player to screen the movie. Anna and Simon resolutely refused to buy a DVD player, instead holding on to their old, obsolete VCR, so Jason rented one for the evening. He hooked it up quickly and skillfully and it was ready for action in no time. Kathy produced a small disc as if by magic from her laptop case. Popping it into the player, she settled on the couch, all four of them, a close family brought even closer by ongoing tragedy. The opening scenes of the video appeared on the screen and they all fell silent.

23

Typha moaned and stirred on the hard, narrow cot. The cell was small and she barely had room to stand and turn around, so she spent most of her time in the cell lying on her bed. Most of the time, though, she wasn't in her cell. She spent most of her time strapped into the interrogation chair, subjected to whatever methods the interrogators were using that day.

On the best days, it was just solitude, peaceful, quiet, solitude. The elders and their employees could never understand that being alone could be a good thing and they would subject her to stretches of blissful solitude which helped her regroup and focus her thoughts. Most days she wasn't so lucky.

She sat up, unable to get comfortable on the hard mattress, especially with her bruises and open wounds tormenting her. She didn't know how long she'd been in custody; she knew she had been through ten sessions of interrogation, broken by ten periods of sleeping in her cell, but she didn't think the sessions were uniform in length. Some times she thought she'd been left overnight in the torture room.

She groaned and swung her legs over the edge of the cot onto the floor. She groaned again as her swollen, bruised feet hit the hard floor more suddenly than she expected. She needed to remember to be more careful. She didn't want to cause herself any additional pain, to help them to break her even faster. They seemed frustrated she hadn't broken already and were stepping up the pain quotient.

Yesterday she heard one of the interrogators saying she was her mother's daughter, all right, and she realized at least some of them were the same ones who worked on her mother ten years ago. The realization made her angry and more determined not to give them what they wanted.

While they worked on her, they shouted questions one after the other, not giving her time to answer them. Some of the questions were peculiar and seemed irrelevant and she realized they were there to cause her to drop her guard. Once she answered one question, the gates would be open and other answers would be more likely to come.

She kept her mouth shut, drawing on her memories of her mother, seeing her bruised and broken, refusing to say a word to her tormentors. Typha was finding a strength within herself she didn't know she had and she hoped it would last through the ordeal. She realized she wasn't getting out of here alive. No one ever got out of here alive.

A key turned in the lock of the cell and Typha braced for the coming day. The guards were coming to get her. She shuffled along the corridor behind the guard. To her surprise, they didn't take her to the interrogation room but instead turned down another, smaller hallway.

Typha was taken into a small room furnished only with a wooden table and two wooden chairs and was left on her own. She heard the key turn in the lock as the guards left and then she was alone. What in the world was going on today? She hadn't a clue.

The door opened again and David stepped into the room. He sat in the chair across the table. Catching sight of Typha's bruised and bloody face, he drew in his breath with a gasp.

"Oh, my God!" he exclaimed, before he caught himself and regained his composure. "How are you, Typha?" he said, more formally, as though there were nothing at all unusual in their situation. "Are they treating you well?"

He blushed at the obviously ridiculous question but maintained a look of polite detachment, and Typha realized he was aware they were being watched...or at least listened to. She nodded. She didn't think she could manage to say they were treating her well without saying the wrong thing. Right now was not the time to break down. She needed her strength for whatever was coming next.

"I need your help", David said. "The disease infecting the plants is spreading. It's moved to another species, and I don't understand how that could have happened. We introduced it to that species in our experiments and there was no response, so I assumed it was unable to infect those plants. Yesterday morning, I noticed yellow blotches on the leaves."

"Which species did it move to?" Typha asked dully.

She wasn't sure she could deal with this in her current condition, but she knew it was critical to the survival of all life on earth.

"It was the geranium", David told her. "I double checked the logs you kept during the tests and there was no problem with the geraniums."

"Did you keep the infected plants totally isolated and carefully clean all the surfaces?" Typha asked.

"Yes, I did. I've been very careful with the cultures, too."

David looked worried, and with good reason. If he'd done anything wrong....

Typha believed David had been careful. He was a good, careful worker and wouldn't take any unnecessary risks. But things could happen even with all the precautions. She didn't know how the disease got into the lab in the first place, so it's possible it could still be susceptible to new infections.

The real problem, she realized, was David. He didn't expect the spread because he didn't understand evolution. He didn't know bacteria could adapt to new situations and become a non-stoppable killer if they didn't find something to control it first. Her antibacterial studies were promising, and she thought she was close to isolating something which could destroy the bacteria, but she was interrupted in her work before she finished the tests.

The elders placed too much confidence in David too early, especially since they forbade her to explain evolution to him. The elders didn't believe in evolution and they felt belief in it was responsible for unleashing evil into the world. Because of their unwillingness to accept the basics of scientific knowledge, they were willing to risk the lives of all the people who counted on them.

Typha groaned again, this time from frustration and anger at the fate which could be waiting everyone. Death from asphyxiation would not be a peaceful way to go.

David leaned closer to Typha, his face nearly up against hers.

"I'm not sure if we're being watched", he whispered. She nodded. "I want to do something to help you."

She frowned and shook her head, warning him.

"I can't stand to see you like this. Why are they doing this?" he whispered.

She put her hand on his...the first real physical contact they ever made. She felt him shudder at her touch and withdrew her hand. He was apparently disgusted by the merest contact with her. But still...he wanted to help her, so at least he did have some level of human compassion.

She shook her head again and turned her face away. He understood and sat back, putting the distance of the table between them once again.

"What can I do about the cultures?" he asked. "I don't understand what's going wrong."

Typha struggled with herself, debating internally whether to tell him what he needed to know. She decided it didn't really matter, since her life was effectively over anyway. She might as well do what she could to save the rest.

"It's....evolution", she said quietly. "The bacteria are evolving. It's adapting to a new host and could continue to adapt and infect other species over time."

She spoke quietly, hardly audible even in the small room, and David leaned close again to hear her.

"Evo...what?" he said.

"Evolution. A species changing through generations of reproduction to adapt to a new environment it finds itself in."

"I've never heard of that", David said. "It doesn't make any sense...does it?"

"It's a...forbidden theory", Typha explained. "I'm not allowed to tell you about it. I'm not supposed to know about it. The elders decided two generations ago the theory was wrong and couldn't be taught or talked about. All the books which discussed it were destroyed and no one is allowed to mention it."

Typha moaned as the wounds on her legs began to throb. This was going to be a long day.

"So, if it's forbidden, and all the books were destroyed, how do you know about it?" David asked with suspicion in his tone.

Typha decided she needed to be careful. Incriminating herself was one thing; with the interrogators surely listening in, she definitely couldn't incriminate the rest of the resistance by explaining about their underground hideouts.

"My grandfather told me about it", Typha said. "He went to school before it was forbidden and he learned about it. He told me because he thought it would make an amusing story. When the plants started getting sick, I remembered what he told me. I thought it might be relevant."

Typha was making things up now and she'd never been good at lying. Usually her approach was to defiantly face down questions and not answer those which could get her into trouble. She couldn't do that this time. This was one question which had to be answered, so she made things up as she went along, surprised at how easy it was.

100

All you had to do was stick as close to the truth as possible and throw in a few details about things which were familiar. The rest sort of happened naturally.

David nodded. He didn't understand how it happened but it made sense. After all, hadn't he seen it? The geraniums were not susceptible to the bacteria last week; now they were. Something changed, either the plant or the bacteria. He didn't know enough science to know how either one of them functioned, and he'd been thrown into this job before he felt totally comfortable. He felt good with the technical aspects: adjusting the temperatures, watering the cultures, keeping the sunlight coming in at the right amounts, and so forth. The whys and hows he didn't understand yet, and he knew without knowledge, he wasn't able to manage a lab where something was going wrong.

The elders didn't understand and weren't prepared to listen when he told them he didn't feel ready to operate the lab on his own. They came in and took Typha away. It took him several days to find out what happened to her. She'd been gone two weeks now and he was desperate and scared about what was happening to the plants.

Typha held his gaze. She was going to have to go out on a limb. He wasn't able to handle this situation on his own and she couldn't do anything from here. He needed the resistance to help him. They had trained scientists, but how could she get him in touch with the resistance?

She didn't trust him, and for all she knew he might have been sent in for just this purpose. How could she know? She had no way to get in contact with the resistance and she wasn't going to tell him the location of the rabbit holes. This was too big for both of them.

"Give me a day to think this through. I'll try to think of a plan to save the plants. Can you come back tomorrow?"

David nodded.

"Good. If I can come up with some idea by then, we can try to work out a protocol to contain the bacteria."

David nodded again. He didn't know what to say and he needed to get out of this stifling room where all he could see was her beautiful, beloved face, bruised and bleeding. He mumbled something incomprehensible even to him and rushed out the door.

The guards returned and hustled Typha out of the visitor's room. She shuffled down dark, winding hallways, this time on the now familiar path to the interrogation room. She walked with a firm step, with fresh courage and strength, her mother's face hanging like a ghostly specter in the air before her as she moved.

24

Anna looked up from her microscope as heavy footsteps alerted her to the presence of someone in the outer office. Sighing at yet another interruption, she wiped her hands and went out to greet the visitor. It was Harry. He was pacing nervously when she entered, and looked up as she moved across the room toward her desk. As she booted up the computer, he returned to his pacing without saying a word, without even a brief greeting. Plainly, Harry was worried about something.

The outer door was thrust open and Dean Ryan entered. Harry stopped pacing. He backed slowly away, toward the filing cabinet, where he stood mute, his fingers drumming on the top of the cabinet.

Anna didn't look up but went on with her work. She had long since moved from the air of forced politeness with Dean Ryan and now mostly ignored him unless he spoke directly to her, which he rarely did. He thrust his hand out to Harry, who took it with a nervous laugh and shook it limply, letting it go again as soon as he could.

Harry was not the same person he was before the transformation. He'd taken to heavy drinking, and it showed. He mumbled something to Dean Ryan, apparently meant to be a polite greeting, but totally inaudible and probably incoherent. The dean frowned and turned his attention to Anna.

"So, little miss, you're still here?" he said with an air of amused detachment, as one speaking to a small child.

"Please, Dr. Ryan", Harry was pleading. "She has a Ph.D. She's as educated as you and I, and she's a marvelous asset to this university and this community." This was more than Harry had said to anyone in months.

"She's a woman", Dean Ryan growled, "and as such, she is not supposed to be working in a science lab. She shouldn't be working anywhere. She should be staying home and taking care of her family. She should be having children, like a good American woman."

Anna ignored Dr. Ryan and kept on entering her data. Nothing she said was going to be treated with importance, anyway, so she decided she wouldn't waste her words. The dean moved closer to her desk and leaned over it, his face practically touching hers.

"You don't belong here, and I'm asking you politely to leave before I have you thrown out", the dean said, softly, quietly, but with a sinister undertone that couldn't be mistaken. "Give me your lab keys."

Anna ignored both the men in her office. It required a great deal of self-restraint to ignore the dean. His face was so close she could feel the rough stubble of his five o'clock shadow and smell his aftershave. It made her nauseated. She didn't intend to hand over her keys.

"Where are your keys?"

The dean walked around the small room, opening the various drawers lining the walls, all of which were filled with scientific equipment.

"Are you deaf, little girl? I said, WHERE ARE YOUR KEYS?"

His voice was loud now, which had the odd effect of making it sound less menacing. Anna met his eyes with a steady gaze. He blinked and looked away.

"This is my lab and I am under contract to the university. I am also working on a grant for the federal government and I have obligated myself for another two years of service on this project. The agreement the school entered into when accepting the grant requires them to maintain this lab space for my work. I cannot hand over the keys until the work is completed."

Anna returned to her work but her heart beat so rapidly she imagined the men could hear the thumping.

"You are no longer an employee of the university. I have decided you need to be home with your family and I am asking you one more time to hand over the keys to your lab."

"Until I receive notice from the human resources department that my contract has been terminated and until they have fulfilled the terms of the contract regarding the termination process, I will consider myself an employee of the university. You don't have the authority to unilaterally discharge me."

Anna held her ground. Harry moaned. Dr. Ryan hesitated, unsure of himself in the face of a person who was standing up to his bullying. He wasn't used to this.

"You'll be hearing from the university." Ryan spun on his heel and stomped out of the lab, slamming the door behind him. Harry jumped.

"I can't believe you said that to him", Harry sputtered. "Why didn't you just give him the damn keys? I would have let you back into the lab."

"Because that's not the way I do things", Anna said. "I don't think it would accomplish anything. He has no authority and he was bluffing. I called his bluff. Next time he comes, he won't be bluffing, so I'd better get some work done quickly."

Anna spoke quietly, the calm in her voice belying her anxiety. She couldn't let them see her nervous. She waved Harry out of her lab and went back to work, her day as shattered as her nerves.

In the evening the resistance met again. Things were happening very fast the resistance met several times a week. It was harder because they needed to find a new place to meet every time. It was no longer legal to peaceably assemble, so they had to be very careful. They had to be careful about who they let into their membership because of the threat of spies. They'd been ratted out twice by members they thought they could trust, members who succumbed to fear and cooperated with the authorities. They needed to figure out how to recruit members and maintain trust in each other, while maintaining a healthy level of suspicion that would protect them from treachery.

Anna was still *de facto* leader of the resistance and Ames was now the nerve center of a large underground movement. They would be literally moving underground as soon as Jason and the others he recruited got the new facility finished.

The resistance discussed Anna's new problem. It wasn't unique to Anna. All female professors were being asked to clean out their desks, turn in their keys, and depart quietly. Many of them complied. Some appeared to comply but set up ways to access their materials and equipment, to continue working on whatever grants or other projects they had going. Others, like Anna, resisted outright, holding out for something in writing, something which fulfilled the contract they were operating under. They suspected such documents wouldn't be long in coming.

Morale was low and shock was beginning to set in among the resistance. Anna did her best to raise the spirits, but her own spirits were flagging so badly she felt inadequate to the job. She was looking forward to getting home and into a hot bath.

25

Typha was losing her strength. Day after day of constant interrogation, many of the days unbroken by time for rest, was beginning to wear her down. The visit with David boosted her morale, but another hour in the interrogation chair was enough to weaken her resolve again. She was afraid she was close to breaking. The only thing that kept her going was the constant presence of her mother's face, floating in the air above her like a guardian angel.

Typha didn't believe in angels and she knew her mother wasn't really watching over her, but she took comfort from the hallucination and drew strength from it. The pain was nearly unbearable but she refused to scream or cry. She closed her eyes and once again she was a teenager, standing in this same room, watching her mother undergoing the same torments she now endured.

Day after day they worked her over, trying to break her, hoping she'd sell out the resistance. Day after day they screamed question after question at her, as they were now doing with Typha, hoping in an unguarded moment, she'd answer one of the questions without thinking. Day after day her mother held out, not speaking, not screaming, not crying, until that dreadful day, that final day, when she turned her head and quietly died.

Typha didn't know how long they'd been there before her mother died. Time in the interrogation room becomes distorted, unreal. Hours become minutes and minutes hours, and you begin to hear a clock ticking in your head in a mocking, distorted rhythm which interferes with any attempt to keep track of real time.

Typha listened to the clock. It struck her…maybe that's how Mom did it. Maybe she paid attention to all these strange sounds and images her brain was feeding her and then she didn't feel the pain so intensely. Typha tried. She got some respite from the pain before it came flooding back. Disappointed, she was about to collapse when the sounds distracted her again and the pain went away for another moment or two.

Striving against her own body, Typha realized the pain doesn't go away, not for long, but if she could get these brief moments of relief it might give her enough space to hold out. She concentrated on the ticking of the clock, on the buzzing sound underlying it, and listened. Peace. This time, the pain free state lasted longer, and Typha hit on the secret. By concentrating on distractions, she was able to short circuit her body's defense mechanisms alerting her to the tissue damage by the feelings of intense pain. That's why no one survived the interrogators, because they lost the ability to sense the danger.

Typha shrugged mentally. She had already resigned herself to the knowledge she wasn't going to get out alive. No one ever did. She didn't kid herself she would be the first. If her mother hadn't been able to survive, how would she? She rested and listened to the ticking. She saw the swirling colors in her brain she'd been getting used to over the past several days but now she quit resisting them and lost herself inside the rainbow.

26

Kathy gave birth to a baby girl. Anna was sure it was the most beautiful baby girl that had ever been born. Jason decided to name the baby Cicada. Anna winced. Why, she asked, such a silly name for a pretty little girl? Jason said, well, after all, she's no bigger than a cicada, and I think it's a cool name. Besides, he said fondly, I want to name her something to show I have a mother who's a scientist. Anna grimaced and Kathy chimed in.

"I think Cicada's a dandy name", she said, "but I don't think it'll do well for her in school. Don't you think we could find another name which would be a little more...well...appropriate?"

The wrangling over names went on for half a day, affectionately, until they decided to call the baby Jasmine, a name Anna wasn't fond of but which she felt was more appropriate than Cicada. Simon nicknamed her Mushroom and the nickname stuck. Anna decided her family was crazy, but she loved them anyway.

All their friends threw them a party. It was a truly enormous baby shower, with members of the resistance showing up from all over the world. Anyone who could take time to get to Ames beat a path to the door. Anna was kept busy welcoming friends, many of whom she'd never met in person before, and helping arrange accommodations for everyone. They held the baby shower in the underground hideout so everyone could take a look at it.

The hideout wasn't finished yet, but it was taking on the look of a real home. Jason had discovered some underground bunkers, former government missile sites, and some of them were for sale. He and Simon negotiated and cajoled until the resistance managed to acquire several large bunkers which they fixed up into living quarters. In addition, enormous rooms were carved out underneath the city, and a labyrinth of trails. The rooms were finished with whatever materials they could get their hands on. They wanted this hideout to be livable in case they had to move down there in the future. Today would be combination baby shower and housewarming.

The conversation was self-consciously lighthearted, everyone making small talk and avoiding news of the resistance or other heavy discussions. In spite of it, Anna couldn't help but feel a heavy pall hang over her. All her graduate students, past and present, assembled at the underground party, and the group seemed incomplete without

Carolyn. This death, she thought, could be laid at the president's door as surely as if he'd assassinated her himself.

The party ran late into the evening, the revelers needing respite from the grim realities they'd been dealing with daily for the past few years. Music rang throughout the subterranean chambers. The sound of conversation and laughter in such a strange and unreal setting, coupled with several glasses of champagne, made Anna feel lightheaded. Images, colors, sights, and sounds began to drift around her consciousness, and she lost track of what was real and what was illusory.

She began to wish she could stay in this moment forever, a moment suspended in time, when the mood was carefree, so much more like the old days, the days before the transformation. Soon, however, the guests began to move toward the exits and disperse into the starlit night of the exterior world. Anna and Simon remained until the last guest left and then walked home, hand in hand, just like they always did. The moon was new and the sky was full of stars, lighting their way through the darkened streets of the sleeping town.

As they turned the key in the lock to their small, cozy home, Anna felt a sickening feeling in the pit of her stomach. If only, she thought, if only the child hadn't been a girl. Scolding herself for the treachery of her thoughts, Anna stepped over the threshold...and screamed.

27

David closed the door to the lab and slipped out of the central compound into the swarming, noisy city. The lights in the dome were beginning to dim as he picked his way through the pulsating mass of humanity beneath his feet. He pondered the item he heard on last night's news, the news that the country no longer had room to bury its dead, so all dead bodies would now be cremated and their ashes disposed of.

The landfills long since filled up and were built over to provide more living space for the constantly increasing population. Trash was no longer allowed; David realized he was being subversive just by remembering a time in his childhood when they threw away broken or used up items. Now no one could throw anything away. There was no place left to throw it, and besides, nobody had enough of anything to want to throw it away, anyway.

The elders, pressed for a solution to the problem, denied there ever were places to throw things away or that anything was ever in such abundance it would be considered surplus. The resources which existed now, they insisted, were the same resources which had always existed…in fact, the elders said, in the olden days, there were no such things as resources. It was only through diligent prayer and faith that they persuaded God to provide for the welfare of the population.

David brushed away the nagging doubts and began the exercises he'd created to restore proper discipline to his mind. It was particularly difficult this evening, with the bruised and bloody face of his beloved Typha hanging ominously in the air all around him. The image seemed to accuse him of something, but what was he guilty of? What could he have done differently?

David bit his lip as he considered the events of the past week. Somehow, he thought, I need to find a way to do something. He turned down the narrow street that would lead him home.

Someone grabbed his arm and pulled him out of the darkening street into an even darker alley. David yelped and began swinging his fists in the direction of his attacker. He felt a large hand cover his mouth and the strength of his assailant was evident. David decided the best thing to do was go limp.

In the dimly lit back street, David was dumped onto the ground in a spot that was, perhaps miraculously, clear of any other human being. His assailant towered over him, a large man in a very narrow spot which made him loom even larger.

David tried to stay calm but his heart thumped wildly. His attacker was joined by two other dim figures, also men, also looming large in the dim light. David stayed silent. One of the men, at a signal from the first, held David in order to prevent him from making any move toward freedom.

"Where is she?" the first man demanded. "What have you done with her?"

David remained silent but his mind raced. Obviously this was about Typha. Typha was the only "she" David knew other than his mother and sisters. Although the elders tried to encourage him to select a marriage partner, he had resisted all their efforts. Most of the women he saw on the street were of little interest, pale and quiet, moving efficiently through the chores which filled their day. Typha was the only women he'd ever met who seemed to have any personality at all.

"Are you deaf, or are you just dumb?" the largest of the men demanded. "If you don't tell us where she is, we'll hurt you."

He raised his fists as he spoke but there wasn't any need. David had no doubt he meant what he said.

"Who are you?" David asked. He didn't want to anger this man further, understanding that his very life was in those large hands. "What do you want to know?"

"Who I am is not as important as where she is", the man said. "I think you know who I'm talking about and we're going to stay here until we get the information we need."

David didn't feel this was the time to play dumb or pretend he didn't know what they were talking about. Besides, he suspected these men didn't plan Typha any harm. They might be able to help.

"The interrogators have her", he blurted. "They've had her for two weeks. I was there this morning, checking on her, and she looks terrible. We have to do something. We have to get her out of there."

The words stumbled over each other in his eagerness to enlist their aid. He realized, belatedly, the possibility they were government men. If there was even the least suspicion about the deepening rebellious thoughts he'd been entertaining lately, they could have sent someone to trap him into an incriminating statement. The statements he just made certainly qualified.

The three men backed off and huddled in consultation. Their whispered voices were so low David couldn't hear anything they said, but for some reason he felt comforted. The demeanor of the group calmed him, convinced him they weren't government men out to catch him in an unguarded moment. They'd been taken aback when he said she was with the interrogators; apparently, this was news to them. Although the light was too dim to see their faces, David sensed the fear they were feeling, perhaps because it so closely mirrored his own....

The men broke their huddle and clustered around David. The first man, the biggest of the three, pulled David to his feet. There was barely room in this narrow street for the four of them without standing in single file, but somehow they managed to cluster together in a huddled consultation.

With a start, David realized he was now one of the group, though he did sense some reticence to tell him much. They weren't sure yet. Was he sincere? Or was he simply another guard, skilled at deception, who fed them just enough information to find out their plans? David was acutely aware these men weren't of his world but instead inhabited some shadowy, hidden parallel world. They were too substantial to be ghosts, but in some sense, David realized, they were specters of a distant, long-dead past.

28

Anna was busy with hammer and nails, hanging pictures on the newly constructed walls of their underground home. The rooms were ready and finished. They'd lived underground for about two months, ever since the day after the baby shower, after they walked home in the starlit night and opened the door to find the mangled, bloody bodies of their beloved cats piled together in the middle of their living room floor.

The rest of the house had been ransacked as though the intruders were searching for something. Drawers were opened and their contents emptied onto the floor. Sofa cushions were slit, and the stuffing pulled out and scattered everywhere. The intruders even broke the light bulbs and squeezed the tubes of toothpaste as though looking for contraband secreted in these common household items. Going from room to room, checking the extent of the damage, Anna was glad there was nothing left for them to find. All the books had long ago been moved underground, except for a handful of approved volumes such as the Bible and a couple of hastily purchased copies of The Chronicles of Narnia. All the notes of the resistance were hidden in a number of secure hiding places around the country. She even removed all her research notes from her computer and from her files, stashing them underground with the books and all her other most precious belongings.

Simon called Jason at the airport where he was dropping off some of their visitors. Jason and Kathy hurried back and helped their parents pack up what little of their household goods were still salvageable. They buried Shadow and Snowball in the backyard, innocent victims of an ongoing war against reason and sanity. They stood over the two little mounds, mouthing an *ad lib* eulogy, remembering many pleasant evenings they'd spent in their beloved home, the cats curled up on their laps purring in contentment. The home that had for so long been a cherished refuge from the ravages of the outside world turned cold and hostile.

A little bit of Anna died that night and for the next few weeks she moved through her daily routines automatically, numbly, without translating anything she did into an emotional reality. It was just life and it had to go on, so Anna persevered.

Simon spread the news among the resistance. They weren't the only ones hit that night. All over the country, all the leaders of the resistance were invaded. Fortunately, most of them were at the shower in Ames. Anna shuddered to think of what would have happened if they were at home when the intruders arrived. She had a feeling the cats had been a stand in for the intended victims.

Now Anna was trying to rebuild a home underground, in the subterranean labyrinth Jason and his friends tunneled out. Already some of the tunnels stretched long enough to connect them with other cities and many of the members of the resistance were hard at work on their own subterranean hideouts. The plan was to have an interconnected pathway between all the cities to minimize the amount of above ground travel they would have to do. For now they weren't spending much time underground. They were living their lives as normal, to the extent they could, and keeping their goods and their sleeping quarters in the safety of the earth.

Simon stuck his head into the room. Looking at all the work Anna had done to recreate a home inside the earth, he nodded his head approvingly. He wasn't really interested in that for the time being, however. He had big news and he was fairly bursting to tell it.

"Guess what I got you today, honey?"

Simon was inviting her to play their old game, trying to tease her into a lighter mood with the old familiar banter. Anna gamely tried to go along.

"Let's see, what could it be? Maybe a platypus?" Anna asked playfully, a trace of her old spirit showing through her words.

Simon shook his head.

"Gee, I just can't imagine. Perhaps a skylight?"

Simon grinned and shook his head again.

"Well, then, it must be…a surf board!" Anna announced triumphantly.

Simon was pleased the old game lifted her spirits but he was truly about to burst with his news.

"I bought your prairie", he announced. "It was up for sale by the government and I bought it. I bought it for you, so you can continue to protect it against all the nonsense that's trying to encroach on it."

"How in the world could we afford that?" Anna wondered. "That prairie is 3000 acres of prime land. It had to be more than we've made in the past decade together!"

"Well, I didn't buy the whole thing", Simon confessed. "You're right, there's no way we could afford it. But I was able to buy about 200 acres, and I bought the section with your wetland. Now you'll be able to continue working to keep that wetland intact. You'll be able to protect it because it's your own. One thing the government hasn't done is terminate the concept of private property!"

The government had actually expanded the concept of private property, selling off all the nation's forests, prairies, and historical sites to private investors. Even the White House was on the block and rumor had it the president planned to buy it for his private residence.

Anna fell silent. She had no words for the enormity of the emotions surging through her. She couldn't express the depth of her love for this incredible man, this marvelous, loving human being who put all others to shame. She sat down and cried, for the first time in a long time, tears of incredible joy mixed with deep sorrow. Tears for love, tears for loss, tears for fear all welling up and unable to be held back anymore, as Simon sat on the couch beside her holding her hands in his. They sat wrapped in the comfort of a familiar embrace as the shadows lengthened and the day grew late in the distant world above their heads.

29

Typha barely lifted her head or made any acknowledgment as David walked into the visiting room but she sensed something changed. David was nervous. She had never seen him nervous; he usually exuded an air of serene confidence eerily similar to the elders. His unswerving confidence in himself and the world around him was one reason she was not able to bring herself to trust him. People with that sort of confidence usually had nothing to hide, and in this world, if a person didn't have something to hide, they weren't someone to be trusted.

David was appalled at the sight of Typha. After the bruised and bloody visage he'd seen yesterday, he didn't imagine it could get much worse but the woman he was now looking at bore little resemblance to the woman even of yesterday. Dull and lifeless, she didn't even have enough spirit left for anger or fear. It was like she just wasn't there anymore.

He realized they'd have to do something quickly or she'd be gone for good. Even if she physically survived the ordeal, it appeared her soul was fleeing her broken body and that might be a lot harder to restore than physical health.

David shuddered. He could hardly bear to see this but he realized it had to be him who presented the plans they'd made. He not only had a reason to visit her, he had the trust of the elders, so he was allowed to visit. The little he learned from his companions of the night before made him acutely aware no one would ever allow Aspen, Annapolis, or Drysdale to visit and then walk out again.

Typha didn't say a word but she was acutely aware of her situation. Her mechanisms for avoiding pain were still at a stage where they could be turned on or off at will, and she wasn't checking out on the world yet. She wasn't sure how much longer that would be the case, but for now she could still remain alert and ready. That was the one reason she was unable to lift her head to look at David; the pain throbbing throughout her skull and her spine was relentless.

She sat with bowed head, her long hair falling over her bruised face, and listened while David engaged in small talk for the benefit of the guards who were still in the room. As soon as the door closed behind the guards, his demeanor changed, his relaxed posture was laid aside, and his voice grew urgent, though much lower than his previously casual tone.

"Here", David pulled a small vial out of his pocket and passed it to Typha under the table. Her hands clasped around it but she didn't make any move to see what it was. "Aspen sent you some pain killers. Keep them hidden. You don't want to have the guards or the interrogators see them."

Typha made a sudden move of her head but regretted it as spasms of throbbing pain shot through her body.

"Aspen?" she whispered. "You've seen Aspen?"

For just a moment she dared hope again. Aspen was looking for her, he knew where she was, he'd come save her. Then dreadful realization set in.

"You must tell him not to come here. He must stay away. He can't save me and he'll only bring trouble on himself and the rest of the resistance if he tries."

David nodded. "He knows that. He needed to know where you are and I was the one who could tell him. He won't be coming here, but he and Drysdale have been in contact with me. We're working on a plan to get you out of here, but seeing you today, I'm afraid we might not have much time left."

Typha again felt a surge of hope mingled with surprise. David was one of them? King David wasn't a product of the council of elders? She tried to think back over the months he'd worked with her and find any clue which would have told her that. She didn't know if it was her throbbing head or simply a faulty memory, but she couldn't recall a single conversation or word between them which would have given her a clue to his fraternity with the resistance.

"I don't know what's going on", David was continuing, "but I do know I'm convinced these men have your best interests at heart. I'm going to try to help them, if you'll let me."

Typha needed to make a decision. She explored all the possibilities. David was one of them from the beginning. David was not one of them but was sympathetic to their cause. David only now discovered their existence and was trying to decide how he felt about it. David was one of the loyal and was simply attempting to lure her into a trap to compromise the rest of the resistance. With a return to her characteristic sharpness, she came to a decision. She couldn't sacrifice the resistance.

"You need to leave, David", she said. "No one can get me out of here now and I'm not sure I want to get out. If I've done anything to compromise the health and wellbeing of the society, and undermined the authority of the elders, I should be isolated and rehabilitated."

Years of working in government service had given Typha the ability to spout loyalist gibberish which sounded sincere and appropriate.

"Nonsense", David muttered. "You're either delusional or you're worried about my status. I can't blame you. You have no way of knowing if I'm honest or if I'm attempting to trap you into revealing information. I have to admit the same thought crossed my mind, that Aspen is actually a guard trying to lull me into a false sense of security and get me to reveal something incriminating. I've felt for a little while that the elders are suspicious of me, though I've never given them any reason that I can see. I realized Aspen isn't one of us, nor is Drysdale. They're...I don't know what...they're something else. From some other world, some other place, a world that exists only in shadows but is as corporeal and solid as anything I've ever been used to...perhaps more."

Typha didn't answer. She didn't know what to say. The idea of escape and freedom was tantalizing but the risks were too high. The resistance would be able to go on without her. It continued after the loss of her great-grandmother and after the loss of her mother, both of whom were bigger players than she was. There was no call to jeopardize the resistance to save one life. So many had fallen. No one had ever been successfully rescued. Slowly, carefully, Typha shook her throbbing head.

"You mustn't do anything foolish", she whispered. "You mustn't let anyone else do anything foolish."

David nodded. He had no intention of heeding her advice but there was no point in arguing with her right now. The time to argue would be when the plan was in place and they were ready to bring her out. Besides, any knowledge of definitive plans might be dangerous for her and for all of them. With the interrogators working on her at every minute, it was probably best she know as little as possible.

Briskly, efficiently, he turned to the business at hand. The plants, he said. I don't know what to do about the plants. I've isolated all the diseased ones, but I don't know how much longer I can prevent the spread.

The change of subject was a relief to Typha. She talked for twenty minutes, outlining a plan which might prevent catastrophe. It was similar to the one she outlined to the elders earlier, and which they interrupted by her removal and arrest. David listened intently, determined he'd understand everything she told him so that he wouldn't fail. His time up, he took his departure.

The guards collected Typha from the visiting room, but not before she had time to secrete the pain killers. They examined her person before they removed her from the room but they didn't find the vial. There were few safe places but she had learned enough about the search techniques to know the places they wouldn't search.

As the guards led her down the hallway, she realized with relief they weren't taking her to the interrogation chambers. They were taking her to the room where she would be left, perhaps for hours, in total silence and solitude. Funny, she thought, how little they realized the rejuvenating effect solitude and peace had on her. How ironic that a technique designed to break her was instead the very thing which helped her hold on.

As she settled into the quiet room, her hands slipped into the secret spot where she stashed the pain killers. No one would disturb her here. She swallowed a couple of the precious tablets and within minutes the throbbing eased. She soon fell into a deep, refreshing sleep.

30

Anna was locked out of her lab. It had been only a matter of time before they decided to just change the locks. She had anticipated this and moved all her things out of the lab and into the underground site. Her office was emptied and the locks also changed on that door.

Anna was now officially unemployed. Her contract with the university had been broken but there would be no union protest since the union no longer existed. All unions were declared illegal in the last session of Congress before they themselves were disbanded by executive order. The country was now being run by a council of elders and the president served at their dispensation. She figured he wouldn't last much longer, either. The president was useful to the elders and allowed them to stage this bloodless coup, but now he was merely a figurehead. After the last election, in which he received 100% of the vote, he was no longer trusted and they would have to get rid of him soon, too.

Anna and Simon were settled in the underground hideaway, along with Jason and Kathy. Jasmine was beginning to crawl and it was obvious she would live out a substantial portion of her childhood underground. Anna ached for her, remembering her own childhood of carefree romping in freshly mown grass, catching frogs and lizards and letting them go again, rolling down a hill covered with flowers, all her friends rolling down beside her.

Jasmine would have a different childhood, without the simple joys of nature hikes and bicycles. Anna vowed she would do her best to make up for the loss by taking her to the prairie as often as she dared. They made their first trip last week, on a trip to check the progress of the wetland. Jasmine was too young to get anything out of it, but Anna believed it was important for a child to smell the fresh air once in a while. Kathy agreed and accompanied them on the short trip.

Anna's visit to the prairie wasn't all pleasant. Much of the original 3000 acres had been sold to developers and was partitioned off into housing subdivisions designed to hold the nation's rapidly swelling population. The wetland itself looked smaller and more fragile than ever and a worrisome black scum appeared on the surface in places, testament to the increased pollution encroaching on the natural system from the rapid urbanization. Anna made some quick notes and spent much of the week devising a scheme for protecting the wetland from toxic runoff. Now it looked like she had nothing but time to put it into action.

After leaving her university for the last time, Anna headed to a small, unobtrusive spot where she would be able to access the underground living quarters. Jason's contractors built several of these in places which combined easy access with secrecy. Most of them led straight down, so it was necessary to set up a system of soft landings at the bottom of the entry. Kathy dubbed them "rabbit holes" and said she always felt like Alice in Wonderland when she entered the place. Getting back out was more difficult, but a member of the resistance devised a series of lifts to carry them back to the surface. Because they required someone at the bottom to operate, they weren't a good option for going down because they couldn't spare someone to always be waiting on arrivals.

The area below ground was growing rapidly and beginning to take on the feel of a community. Similar underground towns sprang up all over the country, peopled by intellectuals, artists, and other free spirits who chose not to conform to the new way. Workers were doing their best to connect as many of these towns as possible in a vast underground labyrinth which would preclude the need for above ground travel in emergencies.

Jason was in the library portion of the underground town sorting out books when she arrived. He'd just received a new collection and he was attempting to catalog it and get it properly stored in some of the empty bookshelves, which would then be labeled with the name of the person to whom those books belonged.

"Look, Mom", Jason said as she poked her head in to say hi. "We just brought in a new collection. This fellow has all the works of Freidrich Nietzsche in the original German. I'll be all week getting this collection stored. There must be 5000 volumes here!"

Jason turned back to his work, humming as he sorted and stored the books. Like his mother, he had a life-long love affair with the written word and the recent fires destroying so much exquisite literature alongside the usual commercial pabulum created a wrenching agony for both of them.

Kathy was in the large meeting room with Jasmine on her lap, reading *Green Eggs and Ham* out loud to a delighted audience of children ranging from a few months to a few years old. These were the children of the resistance and they were being raised in an atmosphere of fear and secrecy which no one considered healthy. The members of the resistance took turns trying to maintain a sense of normality. Today was Kathy's turn. These children were going to be the future, and the kind of future would depend a great deal on the success of the resistance.

Anna snuck up behind Simon and wrapped her arms around him. He turned into her embrace and held her close as she gave him the news of her new status. He knew this was coming and he dreaded it. Anna wasn't the sort who would be able to ease painlessly out of the working world. He was glad the leadership of the resistance devolved unofficially onto Anna; it would give her something to keep her intellectually and physically stimulated and might keep her, at least temporarily, from collapsing into a depression at the loss of her job. Meanwhile, life had to go on, even though it now went on deep underground.

31

David stood before the council of elders. It was the first time he'd ever been in this room and he looked around curiously. He found the central compound fascinating in its utter emptiness, its lack of swarming humanity, and its peaceful silence. All his life he'd been surrounded by noise and chaos and he found the silence strangely refreshing and relaxing.

Right now, however, he wasn't relaxed. He was scared but forced himself to appear supremely confident and relaxed. Nervousness was a trait which could get you in trouble with the elders. They always believed nervous people had something to hide and showing his nervousness could arouse their suspicions. He thought about Typha and her utter composure whenever she went to face the elders. He attempted to channel some of her strength, and stood tall and proud at the rostrum in the front of the room even as he stared down at an intimidating line of elderly men who were all frowning at him.

"What do you mean, this is a potential catastrophe?" growled Elder Samuel.

He didn't like the sound of this, a young man they all trusted and liked coming in and telling them the plants were dying. This was not good news and the council didn't like to hear anything but good news.

David steeled himself and gazed calmly at the old man. "Sir, if the disease spreads any further, the plants will die. If the plants die, we won't have any further options. We don't have the ability to make oxygen and the human body requires oxygen to survive. We need to find a way to contain the disease, and so far nothing is working. The bacteria have spread to three other species that weren't originally infected." He spoke carefully, proud of his newfound command of scientific terminology and his hard won understanding of the important role of plants in maintaining the human species.

Elder Daniel pursed his lips and narrowed his eyes to tiny slits in an attempt to appear as intimidating as possible. He stared at David and David stared back, his cool gaze belying the erratic and traitorous beating of his heart.

"How could that be?" Elder Daniel demanded. "The report we have here indicates that none of the other species were susceptible to the bacteria in the initial round of experimentation. If they're not susceptible, how can they be getting sick?"

All the elders glared at David now, challenging him.

"Sir", he began respectfully. "I've thought and prayed about that very deeply, and I'm convinced God is testing us."

He held his breath as he watched the reactions of the elders. All of them visibly relaxed. It appeared this was going to work.

"The bacteria are God's way of letting us know he is still in charge of creation and he can alter creation as he sees fit. I'm equally convinced he will send us the answer if we have faith and if we listen to what he's trying to tell us."

The elders applauded and David relaxed and breathed normally.

"I knew you were the right man for this job, David", Elder Paul was saying. "You understand the world. Few are able to so cogently and coherently express the wonders of God and his mysterious plans. You'll go far, my boy."

The elders waved him out of the room but told him to wait in the hallway. They needed to discuss the situation he laid before them and come to an agreement on the proper next step.

An hour later, David left the council chambers with a lighter heart. The elders managed to come up with a solution that not only was the most sensible and likely to succeed, but which was exactly what he wanted them to do. They consulted with God and he told them the proper course of action was to free Typha and bring her back to the lab. God, they told him, was pleased with the rapid way they responded when He told them to remove her, and He was pleased with the level of rehabilitation they administered, but now it was time to return her to the lab. He wanted her back at her post until further notice.

David almost skipped out of the room but decided such elation would be unseemly and might make them reconsider their decision. Although he couldn't let them see it, a song went through his heart. Typha was coming back.

32

The crowd outside the theatre fidgeted. They were expecting to see a play, and they weren't happy about being left standing in the rain outside a locked door. It was close to curtain time, very close, and still the doors hadn't opened. No one was sure what was going on but rumors were beginning to start up that the theatre had been closed down by the police.

A rumble coursed through the crowd and grew louder. This was the third venue the play had been staged in over the past four weeks. The police kept shutting it down and the producer kept moving it. If it was closed yet again, would there be any other place to move to?

The door was flung open and the tired, wet crowd poured into the theatre. The box office worked quickly, hoping they could get the curtain up on time in spite of the delay. Jason watched from behind the curtain as the theatre began to fill. It looked like another sold out performance and he smiled.

The continued good attendance at the play in spite of the constant changes of venue and the harassment by the police was a good indication the resistance wasn't alone in their dissatisfaction with the new structure of society. The play was a satirical look at the new society and it pulled no punches in exposing the bankrupt thinking that had gone into the new rules. The new council of elders which replaced the disbanded Congress expressed their displeasure with the mocking tone and lack of reverence and respect played out in the theatre every evening, but in spite of threats and even arrests, the theatre filled up night after night. Jason felt he was finally able to have an impact and help out all the people who worked so hard to restore sanity to the chaos.

It looked like another move was in order but the threat of closure he'd been served with had not yet been fulfilled. This would probably be their last night in this space, and Jason was mentally flipping through his list of contacts to try to identify another location. So far he'd always been successful and the closings hadn't prevented a single performance. At least this was the last performance this week, so he'd have a couple of days to find another spot and get the sets and costumes moved in time.

Jason started in surprise and anxiety at a footfall behind him. Spinning around, on the defensive, he relaxed and grinned as he recognized Bryce, his leading man.

"Are you ready for another big night? Looks like another full house."

"I was worried", Bryce admitted. "With all the policemen hanging around today, I was afraid we'd be locked out again."

"We will be", Jason said cheerfully. "This time, though, they did me the service of giving me a day's warning by their prowling around. I'm already working on another place for next week's performances. I guess after two weeks in this spot, it was too much to hope we'd get another week. It seems our rulers are afraid of art."

"Well, artists have always been subversive...particularly poets and playwrights."

"Yes, and musicians, too. We can't have creative minds out there expressing ideas that might get people thinking. Thinking people are harder to herd."

Jason grinned and shared a high five with Bryce. He considered himself lucky to have him in the play, not only a good actor but a good friend.

Jason had been producing this play for nearly a year now. They'd traveled, carefully and secretly, from city to city, and played all over the country. They had offers to play in Europe but so far hadn't been able to find any way to get out of the country because the elders suspended international travel. It was hard enough to get permission to travel around within the country; travel overseas was strictly forbidden.

He managed to get the script out thanks to the network of computers they hooked up. International communication was beginning to fail in the above ground society as the elders quashed all "unnecessary" education and information, but underground messages traveled rapidly around the world. Many of the country's best minds were now underground and innovation was driven by desperation.

He received word this afternoon that the play had gone into production simultaneously in England, France, Switzerland, Germany, and Latvia. They were going to stage an opening performance which would begin at precisely the same moment in all the countries. He'd also heard theatre companies in Australia and

Egypt were interested. Even another threatened lock out couldn't spoil his evening.

Much of the world looked on with shock and horror at the changes taking place in the United States. At first their allies thought it was some sort of short term aberration and everything would get back to normal quickly. After Congress was disbanded, they were no longer able to believe that.

The assassination of the president made it clear things had gone further than anyone imagined, especially since the assassin operated in broad daylight and was given a commendation by the council rather than a trial and punishment. The council simply grew tired of the president, who began to believe he was selected by God to lead the country into the transformation and beyond. The council regarded him as merely a tool, a popular spokesman who could bring the transformation to pass but was supposed to step aside and turn everything over to the church. Once the transformation occurred, however, he proved difficult to get rid of and assassination seemed the only option.

The initial shock the country felt quickly gave way to numb apathy as the citizens moved into their new roles and seemed to forget about old ideas like freedom and democracy. That was when Jason decided it was time to use the power of the theatre to remind them of what they once valued.

Curtain call brought a standing ovation as the audience cheered and clapped for nearly two full minutes. The actors took their bows and basked in the warmth of approval. This was a good night. The performance went smoothly and the audience was appreciative, forgetting and forgiving the long, wet wait in front of the locked theatre.

Even before the audience was out of the theatre, Jason and the crew began breaking down the simple sets and boxing up the costumes to move. They'd gotten good at the rapid disassembly process, because they knew by tomorrow, the doors of the theatre might be locked against them and they wouldn't be able to recover any of the gear. They stashed it in a nearby tunnel of the underground labyrinth where they'd be able to access it easily once they found a new spot. Jason locked the door of the theatre and headed for home.

Anna was waiting up for him. She always liked to hear how the evening went and she was as excited as he was about the success of his subversive new play. The newspapers were clamped down long since and the independent magazines closed and shuttered. The television played little but church-sponsored propaganda and the radio was even worse, with little but sermons to offer day in and day out. Theatre remained one of the few avenues of communication with the outside world, and the strategic use of theatre brought many new members into the resistance.

Anna was proud of Jason and never hesitated to let him know it. Meanwhile Kathy was making documentaries about the underground movement and dispersing them through a network of friends who broadcast them all over the world. The resistance, an underground secret, was nonetheless well publicized.

"Have you heard the latest news from Europe?" Anna asked Jason as they sipped hot chocolate in the large kitchen which served so many members.

"I heard they're getting ready to perform the play in a spectacular, simultaneous opening night in several countries. Is that what you meant?"

"Not really. I hadn't heard that. Congratulations!"

Anna was effusively enthusiastic. This was the best news she'd heard for some time and she wondered whether this was a good time to tell him the rumblings she heard through the network. Shouldn't he have at least one evening to enjoy his success? She sat silent, trying to decide what she should say. Steeling herself, she decided she'd take the plunge.

"The news this evening was full of reports from all over the world about the fear they are about to be out-numbered by out-of-control, extremist Americans. The European Union has urged its member states to undertake a program of population increase to mirror the population increases occurring in America, in Africa, and in South America. All the progress that had been made on stabilizing population over the past decades is about to be thrown into reverse. The member states were nearly unanimous, with only Germany voting against the new policies. I'm afraid we've lost the last bastion of sanity that remained."

Jason bowed his head in despair. Perhaps it was too late for his play to have any impact. Perhaps he'd been wrong and art couldn't make a difference anyway. He began to feel like he was swimming upstream.

Anna saw the defeat in Jason's posture and she wrapped her hands around his.

"Don't worry, Jason. This isn't set in stone yet. Europe has been much more resistant to this craziness than the rest of the world, and I'm confident they'll put on the brakes before they get too far along. It's just been difficult for them, with the information shut down and the wild stories coming out of Washington."

Jason hoped she was right but he wasn't convinced. It didn't help that he could tell from her voice she wasn't convinced, either. He looked at her closely and was shocked to realize how old she was beginning to look. The last few years were beginning to take a toll on her. She wasn't exactly a youngster any more. She'd been 50 when this all started, and she'd been working nearly non-stop since. She'd become the leader of the resistance by virtue of her unflaggable energy and her commitment to preventing the madness, and that meant a lot of long days and short nights. She'd been through too much, he thought, and if there was anything he could do to ease her burden he was going to do it.

"Mom, you're the greatest", he said, squeezing her small hands inside his large one. "Please get some sleep. You look exhausted."

Anna agreed to go to bed but once in her room beside Simon with the light off, she found she couldn't sleep. Sleep brought nightmares, nightmares which mimicked the strange events of the long, eventful days. Nightmares which burned like fires in her mind, consuming her energy, draining her. Exhausted, she tossed and turned all night, waiting for the morning to bring another endless round of activity.

33

Typha barely lifted her head as the guard entered the room. She'd been in sensory deprivation most of the day yesterday and she found it calming. She learned so many ways to divorce her mind from the pain and discomfort the real world barely made an impression on her anymore.

She knew she was slipping away and was in danger of losing contact with herself, but that didn't seem as important as protecting herself and everyone else against the designs of the interrogators and the elders. She wasn't even sure if she existed anymore. She obviously hadn't died but she felt like she was gone. She'd never believed in Cartesian duality, in a mind that was separate from the physical body, but now she wasn't so sure. Her body felt vacant; her mind seemed to be missing. When the guards came to hustle her out to the visiting room, she was barely even aware of the walk.

David watched her shuffle in, head down, eyes closed, looking like a shell of a person. He fumed at what had been done to her; yes, he was angry. Angry at the elders, angry at the interrogators, and angry at himself. How many people had this happened to?

He asked himself over and over again how he could have been so oblivious to what was going on around him. He'd spent most of his life accepting what he was told about the world, about the people around him, about everything. Now he began to suspect much of what he'd been told was a lie. He could see the lie mirrored in Typha's dead eyes and shuffling gait.

The guards lowered her into the seat opposite his. It appeared she wasn't aware enough to even sit by herself. The guards disappeared out the door leaving him alone with a woman he barely recognized.

"Typha?" he asked gently. "Typha, are you there?"

She nodded but he wasn't sure if she was acknowledging his presence or merely giving a reflexive response.

"Typha, I've got some news for you. You're coming out of here with me. You're coming back to the lab. You're going home."

He searched her face for any sign of understanding. There wasn't even a flicker. She remained silent and motionless, her long hair limp in front of her bruised face.

"Typha, can you walk out with me?" She nodded. "Come on, let's get out of here."

Typha sprang to life. She jerked as though shot with a volt of electricity and brought her head up to stare into his eyes. The sight of her bloodshot eyes was more disconcerting than the bruises mottling her skin. Her gaze was the steady gaze he remembered, the steady gaze so many found disconcerting because it seemed to see right through you and find out all your weaknesses, all your dirty little secrets.

"I told you, I'm not going to escape. I'm going to stay here, and see this through. Escape is not an option."

In spite of her resolute words, Typha was shaking inside. The idea of leaving interrogation behind and walking out of here forever was tempting, but she knew she couldn't betray the resistance. She couldn't lead this man, or any other, to their hiding place. Her eyes blazed with a fire that burned straight through into his heart.

"We're not going to escape, Typha. We're going to call the guards, ask them to open the door, and then we're going to walk out of here. I have your release papers, signed by Elder Samuel. You've been released."

David watched her closely. Did she believe him? She seemed to be convinced he was leading her into a trap. Would she follow him?

"That's not possible", Typha said. "People don't get released except by death. Interrogation is forever. There is no parole."

She choked, remembering the pale face of her beloved mother breathing her last in that horrible interrogation chair.

David wished he knew what she was thinking. She seemed so far away, staring back into a past he couldn't even imagine. Where was she from? Who was she? How did she become who she was, a woman defying all tradition to be something more, even more than any man he'd ever known? He thought about the men in the narrow street, men who were also different, men who moved in a different world than the one with which he was familiar. Typha was from the same world, he was sure. But what was it? *Where* was it?

"Typha, this is different. The elders consulted God and have been told God is done punishing you and wants you released. God wants you to come back to the laboratory and save the plants."

David held his breath. Would she understand? Slowly she nodded. She understood.

"God was testing them and now He's infected the plants with these terrible bacteria as a further test. Only you can save the plants.

You have to come back to the lab, otherwise all the people on earth will die."

David didn't know quite what he was saying. He felt like he was babbling, and the explanation he was giving her felt foolish, childish. For the first time in his life he found himself wondering, is God real? If so, where is He?

He decided not to think about that right now. He needed to get Typha out of here. He took her by the arm and helped her stand. As if on cue, the guards appeared and helped him get her to her feet. One of the guards held the signed document Elder Samuel gave him, authorizing her immediate release. Hopefully they wouldn't doubt the signature because it could delay the release, and there wasn't much time to spare. The guard nodded at David and motioned them toward the door.

Slowly, with David holding her up on one side, and a guard holding her up on the other, Typha moved out the door and down the long, dark, winding corridor. Soon she would emerge back into the artificial light of the dome. Soon she would be able to retrieve her mind from whatever strange dimension she banished it to and then she would be once again whole.

34

Anna breathed deep, the fresh air reinvigorating her. She'd been underground all week, not able to get up into the fresh air. There were so many people arriving who had to be accommodated, so many who wanted to be part of the resistance, who wanted no part of the transformation, she rarely got time to relax. It was incredible to see how many people were showing up, people she'd never dreamed were anything but strict conformists.

Looking around the packed meeting rooms, Anna wondered. If these people had been more outspoken about their disagreement with the way the country was heading for the past few decades, would it have been possible to stop the take over? For at least two decades, Anna and Simon openly resisted the dominant paradigm, speaking out about the dangers of the growing fundamentalist movement, but they were like voices crying in the wilderness. Scattered groups of freethinkers, atheists, agnostics, and other secularists around the country spoke ever more urgently about the threats the Christian dominionist movement posed to civil society but most people responded either with hostility or with a yawn.

Anna always suspected there were a lot more of them out there, but for the most part they were complacent in their freedoms and didn't believe such a thing could happen. Now it had, and they were unprepared.

Brushing that from her mind, Anna sat on the grass and looked around. The prairie seemed more beautiful than ever in the setting sun, and a day in her wetland had done a lot to refresh her spirits. She'd spent the day checking her restoration sites and grabbing water samples. She was determined that, no matter what, she was going to continue her efforts to protect and restore this one small portion of the world.

Simon plopped down on the grass beside her. He and the kids were with her and she was delighted to have their company. There hadn't been many opportunities for them to spend time in the field with her, and she missed the old days when they used to load Jason up in his car seat and spend the entire day working on restorations similar to this one. Now it was even more pleasant with Kathy and Jasmine along.

Jasmine was growing so rapidly, and she was so curious. Anna spent over an hour this morning answering questions about the plants and the wetland and teaching Jasmine a great deal about ecology. She explained about cottonmouths and how to recognize poisonous snakes in general, and she quizzed her on her ability to recognize poison ivy. Jasmine hadn't forgotten a bit of what she'd been taught on the last trek; she soaked up knowledge like a sponge and eagerly asked more and more questions until finally Kathy grabbed her hand and took her off exploring.

"Come on, Mushroom, grandma's got work to do. We need to give her a little time to do it."

Jason trailed after his favorite women, as he liked to call them, much to Jasmine's delight.

Simon and Anna sat side by side in the grass watching the glorious colors of the setting sun. The amount of activity in the rest of the former prairie preserve alerted them it wouldn't be much longer that they would have an unobstructed view of the sunset, and they intended to make the most of the view while they could.

Simon slipped his arm around Anna's waist and before she knew it, they were locked in a passionate embrace, cuddling on the prairie just like in the old days when they were young and dating. The kisses grew deeper and more passionate and Anna felt Simon's hand slip down the small of her back. No matter how long they'd been married, she still felt the old familiar tingle which started in her toes and shot electrical currents all the way through her body. She leaned closer to him, squeezing him in her arms as if wanting to weld their bodies together in a permanent embrace.

A shout alerted them Jason and Kathy were approaching. With a guilty start, like young lovers caught necking in the back of dad's car, they broke apart. Anna smoothed her shirt back down and Simon leaned on his hands, looking up at the orange sky and whistling casually...too casually.

When Jason and Kathy reached them, Jasmine skipping behind, Jason looked at his dad sharply, suspiciously. A small grin came over his face but he didn't say anything. He and Kathy dropped onto the ground across from their parents.

Jasmine raced up behind Anna and flung her arms around her grandmother. Anna recoiled as a snake slithered from between

Jasmine's chubby fingers and landed in her lap. Laughing, she picked up the snake and examined it closely.

"It's a king snake, Grandma, right?" Jasmine queried. She'd been skipping and running the whole way and was out of breath.

"Yes, it's a king snake. Very good, sweetie. You're a good little naturalist."

Anna praised her proudly, thrilled Jasmine was already so good at animal and plant recognition. And relieved – Jasmine never once picked up a poisonous snake and brought it to her. Anna saw Kathy frown and hastened to reassure her.

"Don't worry, Kathy, it's not poisonous. Jasmine is very good at telling her snakes apart, and she knows how to recognize all the poisonous snakes; besides, there really aren't any poisonous snakes in Iowa."

Kathy nodded nervously; she was afraid of snakes and found Jasmine's fascination with them disconcerting. Jason laughed.

"Kathy, here we are, two artists who have a scientist for a daughter. I told you you shouldn't have let Mom read her the *Origin of Species* as a bedtime story when she was only two!"

Kathy laughed, but not convincingly. She was still worried Jasmine would keep on picking up snakes until someday she grabbed a poisonous one by mistake.

Jasmine settled between her parents, snuggling close to her mom. The setting sun behind their heads bathed them in a rosy light, glowing almost like a halo. Anna grabbed her camera and finished off a day of snapping pictures of plants and animals by taking a sunset picture of her beloved family. Jason grabbed the camera and insisted he should take one of her and Simon. Obligingly, the two struck a pose for him, the picture was snapped, and the day was complete.

Carefully wrapping up the leftovers of their picnic dinner, they made their way to the car and headed back to town. For just a short time, it felt almost like old times. Anna could almost convince herself things were back to normal. The feeling would last until they stashed the car in the hidden garage, and headed back to the rabbit hole.

35

Typha was at the table in the lab, patiently trying to explain evolution to David. If they were going to resolve the problem of the bacteria, he would have to understand. The bacteria probably came about from a mutation of some previously harmless bacteria which co-existed with the plants all along. It would be easier, she thought, if she could bring some books for him to look at, or at least draw him some pictures, but because of the illegality of the theory, she couldn't have anything like that in the lab. David put his head in his hands.

"I wish I wasn't so stupid!" he moaned. "I just can't quite get the idea of what you're talking about. It seems like it should be so simple, but something keeps getting in the way."

"What's getting in the way?" Typha asked. "Is it my teaching? I haven't had a lot of experience with teaching."

"No, I don't think it's that. I seem to understand it but I just can't quite wrap my mind around it. I think what's getting in the way is…Genesis. I mean, if what you're saying is true, what about Adam and Eve? If God created Adam and Eve, then God must have created these plant cultures and the bacteria, and it just doesn't seem to work."

Aspen and Drysdale suggested she bring David into the hideout for training. They realized the importance of this, perhaps more than Typha, because Typha wasn't aware that her facility was the only one still remaining to make oxygen. All the other facilities failed and the entire species depended on this one lab, making it truly Central Command. The elders in Ames were pleased when that happened, because it gave them supreme power over all the other councils of elders worldwide, as well as over all the governments run by other religions. No one could live without oxygen so now Ames called the shots.

Drysdale couldn't share their enthusiasm. So much centered in one spot meant a single failure could lead to total annihilation. He hadn't told Typha because he didn't think the pressure would be good for her, but he did understand the grave danger in David not understanding evolution. He urged her to bring David underground. She resisted, still afraid he was a trap the elders had set, but now she decided it was a risk they needed to take.

"David", she started, "I think it's time for your education to be expanded. We need to take you to a new site where I can have the things I need. Will you come with me tonight, so I can teach you properly?"

David nodded, his eyes never leaving Typha's face. Ever since she'd been released by the interrogators, she had an air of fragile sadness which had taken the place of her strong independence. The bruises were nearly healed, and the limp, dull hair matted with blood was once again shining and beautiful, but Typha was changed, possibly forever. David couldn't help noticing the haunted look in her eyes and the way she sometimes looked blankly over his shoulder as though looking at someone standing behind him. He wished he could help her but she still held him at arm's length.

In the early evening, as soon as the lab was locked, she and David threaded through the darkening streets toward the safest rabbit hole. She didn't plan to take him straight there, so she led him on a circuitous route which twisted and turned around on itself over and over before ending up at a rabbit hole about a half hour's walk away from the central meeting area. Even if they were followed, she was sure they probably lost the guards in the teeming crowds which surrounded them. Pausing at the top of the rabbit hole, she took a piece of cloth from her pocket and held it out to David.

"Tie this around your eyes", she commanded him.

David didn't ask questions or protest. He took the cloth she handed him, wrapped it around his eyes twice, and swiftly, skillfully knotted it at the back of his head.

"Good. Now, I'll take your hand. You'll have to trust me."

Before David could assure her he did trust her implicitly, he found himself hurtling through the air, blindly clutching at nothing, hoping to find something to hold onto. After what seemed like an interminable fall, he landed with a thud on a soft surface.

Typha grabbed David's hand and led him through a twisting passageway at a brisk pace. Panting, he attempted to keep up with her but felt like he was being pulled along by an irresistible force. They walked for at least a half hour, by his estimation, and then stopped.

"You can remove the blindfold now", Typha told him, and he yanked it off.

They were in a large room, larger than anything he'd ever seen, larger even than the council chambers. The room was only dimly lit, with candles flickering in sconces on the wall. David had never seen a candle before and stared in fascination and horror. The dim light made the room look spooky as shadows danced eerily across the walls. Typha flicked a switch and the room was flooded with light. David breathed a sigh of relief. Bright light was what he was familiar with, and he felt more comfortable in this setting.

He noticed the room was lined on every wall with enormous shelves. The shelves stretched from the floor to the high ceilings and all along the length of the wall, and were filled to overflowing with books. David had never seen so many books in one place before. He'd been to the school library, where they had a great many books written by accepted and approved authors, but there were nowhere near the numbers that he saw here.

He wandered to one of the shelves and began examining the titles. None of them were familiar. None of the authors were familiar, either. His eye caught sight of a familiar title and he reached for it, pulling the Bible out of the stack. He opened it with reverence, reading to himself. He frowned.

"What have you done to the Bible?" he demanded.

"I don't know what you mean", Typha answered innocently, perhaps a little too innocently.

He glanced at her sharply.

"Then God said, 'Let the earth bring forth grass, the herb that yields seed, and the fruit tree that yields fruit according to its kind…" David read. Skipping a couple of verses, he read "Then God said, 'Let the waters abound with an abundance of living creatures, and let birds fly above the earth across the face of the firmament of the heavens. So God created great sea creatures and every living thing that moves, with which the waters abounded, according to their kind, and every winged bird according to its kind."

He looked at Typha; she had a big grin on her face.

Typha realized the thing that would help David break through Genesis was…Genesis. Bibles weren't forbidden but David had probably never seen a Bible before it was edited and all mention of God creating plants and animals taken out. This was done after the plants and animals went extinct and the elders decided it was better not to mention them again. No one in her generation could remember plants and animals, though she had a vague idea there had still been a few species left when she was born. The final species went extinct less than 30 years ago. The elders re-wrote the Bible but Typha had several translations in her book collection. David had just seen for himself something most people living today had either never seen or didn't remember…this was the breakthrough she'd been waiting for.

Before Typha could comment, they were surrounded. The room burst into life as men and women crowded around David, wanting to get a good look at the stranger. David was used to being surrounded by people and he wasn't bothered by the crowd, but he was disconcerted by the attention. Most people in the streets of the city ignored everyone else; strangers weren't unusual. If you stopped to meet everyone you came across, you'd never get anywhere! Here he appeared to be the only stranger, and everyone gathered around, waiting to be introduced. He and Typha got separated and he glanced wildly around, trying desperately to spot where she'd gone; finally, he spotted a familiar face.

"Aspen!" he cried out, glad to see someone he could sort of consider a friend.

Aspen pushed through the crowd and grabbed him by the hand in a friendly manner. David winced at the strength of the big man's grip. He caught sight of Annapolis and frowned. Funny, he remembered Annapolis as being much larger that night in the alley.

"Aspen, what happened to Typha? I can't see her anywhere."

"Don't worry, old friend", Aspen said, reassuring David. "She's over there".

He pointed to a corner of the room where Typha and Drysdale huddled over some book. David breathed a sigh of relief. He hadn't known what to expect when he and Typha headed underground, but one thing he hadn't expected was to see so many people living like demons under the surface.

Aspen introduced David to the crowd, which slowly dispersed. A handful of people remained, talking quietly among themselves, and David had the feeling he was in the presence of a security system which had nothing to do with the elders…or maybe it did have something to do with the elders, but didn't work for them. He decided he'd better proceed with caution until he found out what was going on.

Typha was back now, sitting on the couch between David and Aspen. Aspen seemed to have lost his friendly demeanor, and scowled as he looked at David. Did it have something to do with

Typha? Probably, he decided. He'd have to be careful. He didn't think Aspen was the sort of fellow you'd want mad at you. He remembered their first meeting in the dark, narrow pathways, and shuddered.

"This is an evolution textbook", Typha explained. "It can explain the theory better than I can, but you'll have to move beyond Genesis in order to comprehend it properly. Just think of Genesis as an allegory, a parable, something not to be taken literally."

She watched David nervously; she had just committed a subversive act and she still couldn't be sure he wasn't a spy. He nodded gravely and began to read. Typha and Aspen moved away, leaving the room together. He was now alone in the large room but the silence didn't bother him. He didn't even realize it, he was so immersed in the fascinating tale unfolding on the page in front of him.

Typha and Aspen stood side by side just outside the door, watching him. They didn't intend to leave him alone until they were sure they could trust him. Typha was acutely aware of Aspen and she could feel the warmth of his breath on her neck. She rested her head against his chest.

"Is he one of us?" Typha whispered.

Somehow she felt Aspen knew him better than she did, although she had been working side by side with him for some time now. Aspen shrugged.

"I hope this isn't an enormous mistake", she murmured softly, every word a whisper, as though cooing soft endearments in his ear.

Aspen simply folded her tightly in a deep embrace and they settled in for a long night's vigil.

36

Kathy's body twisted in pain and Jason hovered as near as he could bear. Anna knelt on the floor beside her, smoothing her hair with a cool cloth in hopes of cooling the fever that had raged for two days. Simon burst in, pulling Dr. Meadows behind him. The doctor glanced took in his new surroundings with an air of detached amusement. Catching sight of the sick woman on the bed, his attention immediately focused and he became all business.

"How long has she been feverish?" he asked the room in general.

Jason answered quickly, obediently. "She first developed a low-grade fever about Wednesday", he volunteered. "This morning, the fever was much higher, and she's in terrible pain."

Dr. Meadows probed Kathy's abdomen; even with his gentle manner, she screamed when he touched her. Jason winced. Anna hustled him out of the room and took him to the kitchen, where she made him a cup of cocoa as they waited for the doctor to finish his examination. Simon stayed behind in case he was needed.

"Mom, I'm scared", Jason said. "I can't bear to think what life would be like without Kathy. She's everything to me. And what would Mushroom do without her mother?"

"Don't jump to conclusions", Anna said. "People get sick all the time and that doesn't mean they're going to die. She's got the best doctor in Ames taking care of her, and he'll do whatever needs to be done. Give him a chance, honey."

After what seemed like an eternity, though the clock registered only a few minutes, Simon and Dr. Meadows joined them in the kitchen. The doctor turned one of the kitchen chairs around backwards and straddled it, a familiar gesture Anna had seen him do in his office many times. It was comforting in its familiarity.

"Kathy has appendicitis", Dr. Meadows announced without wasting time on preliminaries. "She needs to have surgery. I'm arranging to have her taken to the hospital."

A few minutes later Jason and Simon emerged from the rabbit hole, carrying Kathy between them. Anna fetched the car and the men lowered Kathy into the back seat. Jason slid in beside her and cradled her head on his lap all the way to the hospital, cooing to her as she lay twisted in pain and drenched with sweat. Anna maneuvered through traffic with skill, and they arrived at the hospital quickly.

The nurse at the front desk expected them. She came out with a wheelchair as soon as they drove up and whisked Kathy away to the operating room. She waved the anxious family to the sofas in the waiting room, assuring them she'd be back as soon as she had any news.

Anna thumbed through a magazine without reading it as Simon and Jason paced. More than two hours passed before Dr. Meadows appeared in the waiting room, still in his operating gown and surgeon's cap.

"She came through just fine", he assured them, "and she should recover very nicely. You'll want to see her, I imagine."

As they began the walk to Kathy's room, Dr. Meadows motioned to them to be silent; the walk took on a surreal atmosphere. He apparently was more aware than they realized of the changes taking place over the course of the past few years. Kathy was settled into a lonely room in a locked, unused portion of the hospital. As soon as he entered the code to gain them admittance and the big door closed behind them, the silent procession was once again allowed to speak.

He explained as they walked all the security precautions taken to ensure Kathy's safety. Anna and Simon were horrified to learn several patients had been arrested from their hospital rooms by members of the guard which now surrounded the council of elders. They hadn't been aware of it before because most of them weren't members of the underground resistance, and their disappearance was unreported by the church media which was now the sole source of news. As Dr. Meadows realized, the risks in this case were even greater and he arranged an elevated level of security. Jason was effusive in his expressions of thanks.

"Look, friends, you don't owe me a thing", the doctor said. "I'm happy to be of help to anyone who is fighting the menace that's taken over our society and transformed it so horribly. I thought about joining the resistance myself, but I decided I could be more use by remaining behind and keeping my associations intact. There may come a day when the resistance has need of good medical facilities run by people they can trust."

"Like today", Simon said grimly. Anna could see he was more worried now than he'd ever been.

"Like today", Dr. Meadows affirmed, as he pushed open the door to the room where Kathy lay hooked to IVs and heart monitors.

"Here's someone I suspect will be very happy to see you…once she's awake enough to recognize you."

He grinned and slipped away with a snappy salute, leaving them alone with a very pale and sleeping Kathy.

Jason sank on the bed beside Kathy and wrapped both her small hands in one of his large ones. He rested his head on the pillow next to hers and wouldn't be moved. Anna and Simon didn't attempt to budge him. They understood how difficult things could become when you loved someone so deeply.

Kathy recovered quickly and was moved back underground as soon as she could safely be transported. Jason found a trained nurse who was a member of the resistance and was willing to take charge of her care until she recovered. Things began to settle back to normal in the underground living quarters. Anna moved Jasmine to the room beside hers and Simon's so Jason could concentrate on Kathy without having to worry about anything else.

A week after Kathy's surgery, Jason returned from a supply run pale and shaken. While he was out, he stopped by the hospital to leave a message for Dr. Meadows. He wanted to thank him but didn't want to put him at risk by stopping by his office directly.

The nurse on duty at the hospital told him Dr. Meadows was gone. He was taken away two days before; two guards commandeered an ambulance, shoved him into it, and drove off before anyone could react. They hadn't heard from him and didn't know where he'd been taken.

Jason was livid and shaking with rage; he was sure this was connected with Kathy's surgery and Dr. Meadows's failure to go through proper channels. Jason was under no illusions at this point. He realized, perhaps for the first time, the huge sacrifice made on their behalf. He also realized the enormity of the risk to Kathy if she'd been admitted to the hospital officially.

Anna sat in stunned silence. She realized the transformation was serious business and the resistance was taking enormous risks, but until now she never quite comprehended the enormity of it all. She called an emergency meeting of all the members who were present; computer hookups with other cities allowed an international conference.

The news was grim. All over the country, indeed all over the world, people were disappearing, being seized by guards and taken away. Nobody knew where but everybody did agree on one thing. So far, no one who'd been taken away ever returned.

Kathy burst into the conference room, pale and shaken.

"Mom, I'm afraid", she said. "Jason…Jason…"

Breaking off, she ran back toward the kitchen. Anna followed. Jason and Kathy were arguing over something in Jason's hand but Anna couldn't see what he held. Kathy swung away, turning her back on him, and Anna could see what they were fighting over. Jason was holding a gun.

"Jason", Anna said, her calm voice belying the tension she was feeling. "Jason, surely that isn't necessary. We've never needed guns, and we can manage without them now."

"Mom, you know I hate guns. I've never wanted to own one, but now I think it's the only choice we have. We have to arm." Jason's voice shook; Anna realized her calm, collected Jason was afraid.

"I know, we're all afraid. We're feeling helpless right now, and there aren't enough of us to affect a change peacefully. But guns, Jason! What good do you think guns will do? For them to work, you have to be willing to shoot to kill, and you've never killed anyone in your life. You couldn't even take a kitten to the pound to have it put to sleep, and you weren't doing the killing yourself."

"This is a new world, a world where cats are disemboweled and left lying on the living room floor. This is a world where doctors get spirited away from the hospital just for saving a life. This isn't the world you grew up in, or even the world I grew up in. This…this….this is a nightmare world, a world we never dreamed could happen."

"Jason, I WILL NOT tolerate having a gun in the same home with my daughter!" Kathy broke in, her voice uncharacteristically sharp and angry. "I refuse to give in to fear, and I refuse to raise my daughter in a climate of fear. Now take that damn gun back to the store where you bought it!"

Kathy turned away from Jason again, the firm straightness of her back expressing her anger more eloquently than words. Anna was surprised when Jason refused to budge; usually he was willing to give Kathy anything, but this time he was adamant. He was keeping the gun.

"Mom, Kathy, listen to me. We've always had principles, and we still have our principles, but sometimes our methods have to change.

144

Yes, I'm responding to fear. It's natural to respond to fear, to attempt to protect the ones you love when you're afraid for their lives. I shudder to think what could have happened. What happened to Dr. Meadows…that could have been Kathy…that could have been you, or Mushroom, or Dad. I'm afraid, more afraid than I like to admit. I think it's time we have to acknowledge the changed state of things and get ready. We didn't prepare for war…but that's what we're going to get, and it's best to be prepared."

"War!" Kathy shouted. "War! Please, Jason, don't say that."

"Damn it, Kathy, I wish I didn't have to, but I can't pretend any longer. We have a choice…we can prepare for war, or we can give up. We've gone too far to give up and the consequences of the actions we've taken are much bigger than we realized. We thought we'd go into hiding for a couple of months and then things would be all right again. That hasn't happened, and it isn't going to happen. If we want Mushroom to have a future, we have to prepare ourselves to defend that future."

Kathy broke down in sobs. Jason took her in his arms, attempting to comfort her, but it was too late. The truth of his words sank in, not only with Kathy, but with Anna. Despairingly, Anna watched them murmur to each other as she took stock of the situation. Damn, she thought, where the hell is Simon? He should be home by now.

37

David was busy in the lab, logging the latest experimental results. The past few weeks were a whirlwind and he was still not sure how to react to everything. One thing he was sure of: he was now completely a member of the resistance. He made it official last evening when he chose a new, non-Biblical name for himself, to differentiate him from the faceless masses of swarming humanity which peopled the streets above. King David was no more, except in his rapidly fading acceptable, conformist role; he was now Heathrow. He wore the name proudly, even though he couldn't breathe it aboveground.

Before he turned, he sensed he was being watched. Looking up from his datasheet, he noticed Elder Matthew standing just inside the door. He entered silently and watched David as he worked. The elder put his fingers to his lips, signaling David to be silent and padded toward the table, sliding without a sound into the opposite chair. David was startled to realize Elder Matthew was in his stocking feet and immediately he understood. He didn't want anyone to know he was here.

Elder Matthew leaned over, his face nearly resting against David's, and whispered "Where's Typha?"

The elder looked curiously around the lab as if expecting to see her hiding behind one of the strange pieces of equipment, ready to leap out at him. He was plainly nervous and David's interest was piqued. What was going on?

"She's not here right now", David answered in a whisper, understanding without being told that they were exchanging a confidence.

There was nothing wrong in Typha being gone; she just stepped over to one of the other buildings to calibrate some instruments. What was wrong was Elder Matthew being here, though David didn't understand why.

"She had to check on some of the instruments in Building Seven. She should be back in a few minutes."

The elder glanced around the lab, fascinated by the mysterious equipment which surrounded him. Wandering to one of the microscopes, he bent over and peered through it intently as though looking for the secrets of the universe.

"What's this?" he asked.

David answered carefully, not sure what was safe to say.

"That's a slide of a culture we're testing to see if it responded to our antibiotic treatments. We're hoping to find an antidote for the bacteria that's killing the cultures."

Stepping nimbly to the microscope, he fiddled with a few dials, adjusting the focus so Elder Matthew could see more clearly. The older man looked again and then straightened up, his eyes gleaming with a curious light. He looked years younger, like a child who'd just been shown something marvelously new and exciting.

"What am I looking at?"

David entered naturally into the role of teacher, patiently explaining the inner workings of the plant cells they were looking at, showing the old gentleman the various structures and explaining their function in the cell. He slid out the first slide and exchanged it with another slide he'd just made, one with infected cells. He was explaining to him how to tell the difference between plant cells and the bacterial cells infecting it when the door opened, and Typha burst in excitedly.

"Heath….David!" she said, spotting the old man just before she said the wrong thing. "I've just come from Building Seven, and you'll never guess what happened!"

She slipped a slide she was carrying onto the stage of the microscope and told David he needed to look at it, keeping a suspicious eye on Elder Matthew the whole time. David noticed that the elder never took his eyes off Typha but there was a curious look on his face, a look of sadness, almost of….longing.

David frowned. Was the old man in love with Typha? Boy, there were too many men in love with this woman, he grumbled to himself. With reluctance, he directed his attention back to the microscope where Typha waited impatiently.

He bent and looked; it was incredible! The bacterial cells on the microscope were being engulfed by another type of cell. The engulfing cell looked like a bacterium, too. What was happening? He remembered reading about this but he wasn't sure. He'd learned so much so quickly it was difficult to keep everything straight in his head. He looked at Typha with a question in his eyes. She shook her head, smiling. He knew she was telling him it had to wait. He followed her eyes. She was watching Elder Matthew warily as he moved around the lab, looking at first one thing, then another.

147

"What's he doing here?" she whispered.

"He came looking for you", David whispered back. "I don't know what he wants, but he's not wearing his shoes and he's sneaking around. I figure he's not supposed to be here."

Typha sat in the chair David vacated a few minutes before and began checking his data, her heart thumping wildly, pretending to be unconcerned. She did her best to appear absorbed in the data but she was afraid she wasn't pulling it off well. Her head was filled with the Interrogators and her heart thumped so loudly she was sure the men must be able to hear. She jumped when Elder Matthew put a hand on her shoulder. To her surprise, he leaned down and whispered in her ear.

"Is there somewhere we can talk? Somewhere safer than here?"

Typha's chest tightened. She was having trouble catching her breath. All of the fears she'd been keeping a tight lid on over the past few weeks rushed back and she began to feel she was suffocating. She closed her eyes and tried to concentrate on her mother's face, hovering always near whenever she felt stressed out.

She became aware of David shaking her.

"Breathe, Typha, breathe!" David was practically shouting.

She felt herself get lightheaded but she couldn't breathe. David kept shaking her and shouting, but she couldn't focus on his voice. She was losing control, she was slipping away, and her mother's face was shifting, fading, and re-forming into her own. She felt a sharp pain, and she gasped and began breathing again.

"Sorry I had to slap you, Typha", Elder Matthew was saying as she struggled back to awareness. "I was afraid you were about to faint and I needed to bring you back before you slipped away."

Typha's head was swimming and as she opened her eyes, she saw the outlines of David and Elder Matthew only as a blur, melting away before her eyes, reforming, and gradually blending together, then finally solidifying into two solid human forms again. Both of the faces stared into hers with concern. She didn't know what her journey looked like from their angle but obviously it scared them. She shook her head to clear it and felt it throb.

Elder Matthew slipped into the chair opposite hers. He looked at David, hovering with concern over Typha's chair, and asked, "Could we be left alone, please? I have something I need to say to Typha."

David looked doubtful. He wasn't ready to leave Typha alone. He, too, remembered the Interrogators and the bruised and bloody face, the empty eyes. He scowled, a ferocious scowl meant to threaten. Elder Matthew looked amused rather than frightened.

"I'm not going to hurt her. I just need to tell her something and it's something best said to her alone. Give us five minutes; then you can come back in and make sure she's all right. In fact, if you're worried, you can wait right outside the door so I couldn't possibly take her out of here with me."

David bowed his head in a gesture of respect he learned long ago, even before he entered school. This was one of the elders, after all, and even after everything he learned from the resistance, old habits died hard. He stepped out of the lab but took up his station right outside the door, determined to be nearby if Typha needed him. As he stepped out, he gave her a signal to let her know she should cry out if she needed him. She gave him a weak smile, nodded her head, and almost whimpered as the door closed behind him. Now she was alone with one of the elders.

"Typha", Elder Matthew began. "I've wanted to tell you something for years but I never had the courage. There are certain things in this world that just aren't spoken of, and even now, I still don't know how to begin."

He broke off, staring hard into her eyes as though to see through to her soul, but she didn't say a word.

"Years ago, I met a young, beautiful woman, a woman who was strong and independent, not like any woman I'd ever met before. I was a young man, just beginning my life as an elder, and married to a decent woman who was chosen for me as a proper wife. I wasn't supposed to fall in love but I did. I tried to stay away from her, but I couldn't. I did everything I could to be near her. It didn't do any good. She wouldn't look at me because I was the enemy. I wasn't anyone she could ever love."

Typha felt her chest tightening again. She began to suspect what she was about to hear and she didn't want to listen. Her heart screamed at her not to listen but there was nowhere to run. She closed her eyes, tried to escape as she did during the Interrogation, but when her mother's face appeared this time it seemed to taunt her. She opened her eyes and resolutely faced Elder Matthew.

"I kept up my pursuit, even knowing it was wrong, knowing it was against the law, knowing it was against God's law. Eventually my suit was successful. This beautiful, special, and unique woman became my lover. We were together for years, meeting secretly, loving secretly, always fearing it would be our last time together."

Typha squeezed her eyelids more tightly. Her heart kept screaming NO as the words of the elder slammed relentlessly against her brain. She slumped in the seat, whimpering, as the old man continued his story.

"One day she told me she was pregnant. I was terrified. Our secret would be revealed and I would be shamed and ostracized. I begged her to leave me, to go away somewhere and bring the child up far away, even though I desperately wanted her to stay by my side. I was afraid she would be tortured if it was discovered she was carrying the child of an elder. She didn't go away; she stayed here and had the baby, a baby girl. She named her baby Typha...a strange name to my ears, but a beautiful one."

Typha darted toward the far corner of the lab, as far away from the elder as she could get. She careened around the lab without direction or purpose, exhausting herself, and coming to rest against the door. As she landed against the door, she heard David on the other side; the knob turned and she felt the door press against her as David tried to get in without knocking her over.

She put her face through the crack in the door to show him she was alright and told him to give them another minute. He glanced sharply at her, at the despair written on her beautiful face, and hesitated. Her eyes pleaded with him to...what? Come in and get her out of her misery? Wait outside until she called? His heart aching, he nodded and stood silently as the door closed against him.

Elder Matthew had come up beside Typha, and he took her arm and gently led her back to the chair. He waited while she settled, her face turned away from his, her back stiff and straight, before he continued his story.

"I watched the baby grow into a beautiful young woman, also strong, also intelligent. You were educated as a scientist by your mother and never knew me, though your mother and I still met frequently. Then she was captured by the guards and turned over to the Interrogators. I couldn't do anything to save her. I tried, but I realized any interference from me would have endangered you as well. I felt so helpless. I'm one of the council, and still, I couldn't do anything! My rank wasn't high enough. Oh, Mushroom… Mushroom…I'm so sorry. I wanted so bad to save you. I'm so sorry I failed you when you needed me most."

Elder Matthew laid his head on his hands and cried. Typha wasn't sure what to do. This was a dangerous man, she knew that, a man who could have her snatched up and taken back to the interrogators if she said just one wrong word. Her instinct took over, and she stroked his head as if he were a child. The touch of her hand had a calming effect and his sobs quieted. He regained his composure.

"I've always wanted to tell you, Typha, and have a chance to actually be a father to you, but I was afraid it would land you with the Interrogators. When they took you away I tried to come after you but they wouldn't let me in. I don't have the right authorities to command the Interrogators. I felt helpless again, just like when Jasmine was taken away. Then, like a miracle, the plant cultures got sicker, and you were needed. David…well, if it wasn't for David, you probably wouldn't be alive today."

Typha was stunned. All her life she assumed her father was someone from the resistance. She couldn't accept what she was hearing. Her mother had an affair with an elder? Her beautiful, strong, and fiercely independent mother? How could such a thing have happened?

"How do I know it's true?" she demanded. "Do you have any proof you're my father?"

"I knew you'd ask that", Elder Matthew said. "If you're truly Jasmine's daughter, you're not going to just accept it on my authority. So I brought you this…"

He pulled a small package out of his jacket pocket. Trembling, Typha accepted it and began to unwrap the string. Inside the package was a small locket, a locket containing her mother's picture. It was engraved "to my beloved Matthew from his dearest Mushroom". Still…it wouldn't be difficult to obtain a fake, especially for an elder.

A paper fluttered out, a paper written in her mother's own handwriting and dated six months before Typha's birth. It was a letter on resistance paper, the special type of paper they learned to make from recycled materials, a stationary with its own unique signature. The letter informed him of her mother's decision to have the baby, to bring her up underground, and train her in science, literature, and rebellion. Typha cried and clasped the paper to her heart.

Heathrow, hearing Typha cry, rushed back into the room, ready for action. He was puzzled by the strange scene in the room and he stopped dead. Typha huddled on the floor, crying and grasping a locket, while Elder Matthew knelt beside her, tenderly stroking her head and crying himself. This wasn't what he expected at all. Confused, he backed off but stayed in the room, his back against the door, tensed and ready for anything.

Hours later, the three of them were seated in Typha's little room, which was restored to her after her release from Interrogation, complete with book and candle untouched in their pocket in the mattress. Heathrow had been filled in on all the details and Elder Matthew filled in some more details of his own.

Typha was getting a clearer picture of her mother's life in the resistance. Her mother, she already knew, was the first child of the resistance but had been born aboveground just before the final retreat into the underground hideout. She was trained by her mother and grandmother, and as a result had a broad knowledge of both science and the arts. She was the driving force behind the resistance after her grandmother died.

Elder Matthew, it seemed, had sympathy with the resistance. He learned a great deal from Jasmine and what he learned conflicted greatly with his formal education. He, also, was born just before the resistance went underground, so he was brought up in a world being wrenched apart by the transformation. His parents became deeply involved in the transformation and his father was elected to the council of elders.

Matthew was groomed his entire life to be an elder. His education didn't include instruction about the time before the transformation, other than to understand it was an age of darkness and fear. From Jasmine, he learned otherwise and channeled assistance whenever possible to the resistance. That was why the interrogators were so determined to learn the identity of Typha's father. They realized there was some internal assistance coming from high places, and they rightly assumed it was from the father of Jasmine's child. Jasmine died to protect him, to protect Typha, and to protect the resistance. He was not allowed to grieve openly for her loss and he never came to grips with it. He talked slowly, his eyes remaining on the picture on Typha's wall, a picture of a young couple with a child, their heads encircled with light from the setting sun.

In the little apartment, Elder Matthew made his final commitment to the resistance. He said he wasn't going back to the council of elders and requested sanctuary underground. Typha hesitated; was he genuine? She was trained by her mother to be suspicious and her instincts to mistrust always stood her in good stead. She looked over at David...excuse me, Heathrow...and remembered she mistrusted him, too. He turned out to be legitimate and was already proving to be a valuable asset to the resistance.

Typha only hesitated a moment. She knew exactly what to do. She would introduce him to Drysdale, who was a very astute judge of character. The resistance could make their decision as a group. First things first, though.

"Heathrow, would you take Elder Matthew and get him a change of clothes?" she asked. "And make sure you stay with him while he's changing."

Heathrow nodded; he understood. They were taking precautions against tracking devices. Neither of them thought the elders were clever enough to come up with a plan like that; their education had been almost strictly in the ways of the church and not in science or technology. That's the reason they needed to tap into members of the resistance for any sort of technological fix. Still...just in case.

He went off with the older man and Typha leaned back against her thin pillow. She relaxed as much as it was possible to relax with the noise of mindless comedy blaring from the omnipresent television. At times like this, she actually appreciated the constant din. It masked her darkest thoughts and made her unable to concentrate on the shadows threatening to engulf her.

Typha dropped off to sleep. Her dreams were tormented by visions of her mother, the Interrogators, and the council of elders, all moving in and out of her sleeping mind like the strange, wonderful, and scary characters of that old children's book, *Alice in Wonderland*, her mother read to her as a child. She tossed and turned, but in spite of the disturbances which plagued her sleep, she awoke from her nap rested and ready to tackle the night that lay before her.

38

Simon looked up uneasily, with the sense of being watched. He stared straight into the pale blue eyes of the younger man behind him, watching over his shoulder as he cataloged the weapons the resistance had stockpiled. Ever since Adam joined the resistance, he spent much of his time watching other members and Simon didn't trust him. With this very delicate part of the operation, he was particularly uneasy.

"Hi, Adam. Can I help you with something?" Simon attempted to make his voice friendly and welcoming, to make sure he didn't betray the suspicion he felt.

"Naw, just lookin'. I've always sort of had a thing for guns; used to shoot with my old man out in the country before he left."

Simon nodded and continued with his work. It had proven easy, maybe too easy, to get weapons. One thing the new society held to as an article of faith was the strength of an armed populace. Now the store of weapons was drying up and they were rarely able to obtain a new specimen. After the elders realized an armed populace was much harder to control, all weapons were rounded up and confiscated. Like the books, they were destroyed because they were dangerous to the existing order. It proved impossible for the elders to find all of them; many people simply chose not to give up their weapons and were willing to lie, and in some cases, kill, to protect their guns. There were also still people out there who were willing to sell guns, grenades, and even bombs to the resistance.

"Hey, where'd ya get that one?" Adam was admiring an Uzi Simon had just cataloged and set carefully in its allotted spot. "How ya getting' your hands on all this neat firepower?"

Simon went on with his work, acting as though he hadn't heard the question. Adam was too curious, he decided, and it was best not to answer such questions until they were sure about him. Too many people continued to disappear and reports arrived daily about a secret tribunal known as the Interrogation. The council guard that sprang up to protect the elders was known for brutality, but rumor had it they were like a romp in the park compared to interrogation. No one living had ever faced the Interrogators; the bodies of those taken were found later, barely recognizable from the tortures they had undergone. Simon shuddered as he thought about the implications.

"Hey, when ya gonna let me see some action? I'm a great shot, ya know, and I bet I could take out a dozen of those guards without working up a sweat."

"I'm sure you are", Simon answered, "but these weapons are only for defense. We're not using them unless we absolutely have to; we're extremely outnumbered, and going on the offense would be just plain foolish."

"Ah, come on, it isn't about numbers. It's about spirit! It's about believin' you can do it."

Adam wandered aimlessly about the storeroom, carelessly touching first one weapon, then another. As he spoke, he glanced at Simon with a sharp, alert look that belied the carelessness of his manner. Simon's steady gaze met and held Adam's gaze, challenging him to...what? The younger man shifted his gaze, dropping his eyes uneasily. Without a word, he shuffled out of the storeroom.

Anna entered just as Adam was leaving. Casting a glance backward at his retreating figure, she frowned.

"Can we trust him?"

"I dunno." Simon shrugged. "I sure hope so. He already knows way too much about us for comfort if he's not trustworthy."

"He seems...suspicious", Anna said, voicing the concern of the quiet man beside her. "I think we should keep an eye on him for a while."

"That shouldn't be too hard", Simon chuckled. "He spends so much time keeping an eye on us that he's never out of our sight for more than three minutes!"

Anna looked over the array of weaponry collected on the table in front of her. She grimaced.

"Simon, is this really all necessary? Isn't there some way we can manage without having to collect guns?"

"I wish there was, Anna, but I'm not sure we can take a chance. I hope we'll never have to use them."

Anna settled in the easy chair across the room, keeping her eyes on Simon as he went about his work. Ever since the day they found out about Dr. Meadows, Simon was a changed man. The sparkle in his eye disappeared and she rarely heard him laugh anymore. When he returned, he was easily persuaded by Jason that there was a need to prepare for defense. Anna couldn't take it lightly; Simon had always been a peaceful man and never owned a gun in his life. He was not given to paranoia, which made his fear even more alarming.

Although Kathy continued to be skeptical about the need for weapons, she resigned herself to the new order of things. She stayed far away from the storeroom and forbade Jasmine to even go near the door. Jasmine had trouble obeying at first; she adored Simon and was prone to sneaking up on him and covering his eyes with her tiny hands, playing a little game of "Who's there?" After Kathy caught her opening the door to the storeroom, looking for Grandpa, she made the girl swear she would never go there again. Jasmine took her lesson seriously and began studying up on the resistance, attempting to understand why the grownups were so afraid.

There was a commotion outside the door and Jasmine burst in. Anna stood, ready to shoo her out, but Jasmine wasn't being silenced this time.

"Grandpa, you gotta come quick! There's men here, they came down one of the rabbit holes, and they're lookin' everywhere for something. Come on!"

Jasmine grabbed Simon's arm, pulling him out the door so quickly he barely had time to grab one of the rifles from the table in front of him. Anna rushed out behind them to a scene of utter confusion.

Adam stood with his back against the big bookcase. Three council guards towered in front of him, rifles pointed at his chest.

"Where are the leaders of this movement?" they demanded. "Who is in charge here?"

Adam didn't answer; he just gasped for breath, unable to speak or move. The guards continued focusing on him, unable to see Simon sneak up behind them although Adam could see him clearly.

Anna held her breath, hoping Simon wouldn't try anything foolish. He had only one rifle and there were three of them, all armed. Adam whimpered but didn't give them any answers. The lead guard stepped forward one foot, menacingly, and placed his rifle against Adam's chest.

"Well? You were sent here to find the leaders and bring them out. You haven't given us a report in over three weeks, and we want to know why. What you been doing all this time?"

Adam remained silent, clutching at the bookcase behind him. Without warning, his left hand shot out, hurling a giant book directly at the face of the guard holding him prisoner. The guard lunged backwards, losing his balance and falling onto the couch. Adam grabbed the gun as he fell.

As soon as Simon saw Adam's hand leave the bookcase, he stuck his gun in the back of one of the guards. The other guard dropped his gun, realizing that between Adam and Simon he was now surrounded. Anna grabbed the discarded rifle and held it, cautiously, pointed in the direction of the guards. Her hands shook but she held her ground.

The door burst open and a number of other members entered, each of them armed. The commotion alerted them and they took the precaution of stopping by the weapon storeroom to grab a gun. Defeated, the guards were persuaded to take a seat on the couch. Jason brought in a length of rope and tied them up for safekeeping.

Anna and Simon retreated to the kitchen, leaving the prisoners with Jason and the other men. This was a serious business and they needed to talk it over. It was evident they couldn't let the guards go, because they knew how to find their hideout. How many other guards had been alerted to the location of the rabbit holes?

"This is bad, Simon. We can't just let these guys walk out of here."

"I know, sweetie. But we can't keep them here, either. We don't have the facilities."

Adam came into the kitchen, white and shaken but slowly regaining his composure. He sank into a chair and gasped for breath.

"I'm sorry, man. So sorry. I didn't know…when I was with the guards, I didn't know anything. I thought I was going to be fighting evil…I thought I was doing God's work…I didn't know…forgive me. Oh, please forgive me. "

Simon sized up the younger man. The silence seemed interminable but actually only lasted for about a minute. Simon came to his decision.

"We can forgive you, but you have to tell us about the guards. How many others know our location?"

"None, I swear it. I didn't know anyone had figured it out; I think they just stumbled on it by accident, because I was careless the last time I gave them a report and didn't cover my tracks well. That was before I understood, before I realized…." Adam's voice trailed off to a whisper and he began crying.

Anna put her hand on the young man's shoulder, reassuring him, comforting him. She was still suspicious but the best course of action appeared to be letting him talk. She murmured a few words of encouragement.

"Man, I'm so ashamed. I've been terrible, and I don't know how I can make it up to you. I believed everything the guards told me about you. I believed you were in league with Satan, and you were trying to destroy everything that was good and right in the world. I didn't know....I didn't know."

"What made you change your mind?" Simon was quiet but the question was firm. Adam would have to convince them he was serious.

"The books, man, the books. I've never read much before, except my school books, and a few Bible verses. Those books...there's so many ideas there, so many things I didn't know. I had no idea...the ideas are so...incredible. "

"You've been reading the books, and those convinced you?" Simon still held the same quiet, firm tone of voice.

"Well, not totally, no. It was you...you two and Jason. You're such good people, all of you, not like I was taught. You...you trusted me. You taught me. You took time with me and acted like you cared. No one's ever taken time to care about me before. You're...you're for real. You're like family, and I couldn't sell out my family."

Adam sobbed. Anna felt his shoulder shaking under her hand and she tightened her grip reassuringly. She glanced at Simon. He nodded. He believed Adam. Anna smiled. She was sure Adam was being honest and Simon was an extremely good judge of people, so she relaxed a little.

"Now, Anna, we have to decide what to do with those guys in there." Simon turned his attention back to the matter at hand.

"I...I'm afraid...we'll have to...get rid of them."

Anna's voice was tight and small and her face pale. This was not a suggestion she ever wanted to have to make. Simon nodded grimly. The war had just come home.

"I can't do it, Anna, and I know Jason can't. Neither of us has ever even killed a mouse. How can we execute someone?"

"I don't know. It seems so...cold-blooded."

Anna's voice came out in cracked sobs. She knew, after today, they would never be the same. Things were changing and she couldn't keep up with them.

"I can do it", Adam said. "I don't like to, but I'm probably the best candidate. After all, I'm the one who brought them to your door."

Simon glanced at Anna. Anna frowned at him. After all, this was a huge step to take so soon after he admitted to being a spy.

"I don't know..." Simon began. Jason came into the kitchen, carrying the book Adam threw at the intruders.

"Dad, Mom, I know what you're talking about, and I think I know what you're likely to decide. I just want to let you know, I can't let you do it, Dad. I'll take the responsibility."

Jason's voice trembled. The pallor of his normally ruddy face shocked Anna.

"No, baby, you can't do that. I won't let you." Anna was firm.

Simon spoke quietly but with clear authority. He accepted Adam's offer but suggested someone should accompany him for safety's sake. Jason agreed and offered to go along to make sure everything went all right. Jason handed the book he was carrying to Simon. Simon glanced at the title, laughed without humor, and handed it to Anna. The book was *War and Peace*.

Anna and Simon huddled on the couch, tense with anxiety, as they awaited Jason's return. They were worried about sending off a known spy with a gun and their beloved son, but at least Jason took along a gun of his own and a couple of his friends.

Jason returned, followed by his friends, all of them pale and shaken. Simon looked from one to the other; Adam wasn't with them.

"What happened?" Simon asked.

"It was horrible, Dad, just horrible. Adam did the job quickly. We questioned the guards and learned they hadn't told anyone else where the rabbit hole was. They discovered it because of Adam's carelessness and just came down on a whim. They didn't really make any plans or have any back-up. Then Adam did the execution. It was cleanly done, and they died quickly, without suffering."

"Where's Adam?" Anna demanded.

"That's what was so horrible. After he did it, he just stood there for a moment, looking down at the bodies. Then he pulled a handgun out of his pocket, put it in his mouth, and pulled the trigger before we could get to him. He couldn't handle the killing."

"That does it", Anna said firmly. "The guns are going to go. We'll have to take our chances as best we can. We can't let ourselves turn into what we're fighting against. We can't just execute those who disagree with us. If we go down that path we won't be able to turn back, and even if we win, we lose."

Simon looked at the pale faces of the young men in front of him. He felt Anna tremble beside him, half in fear, half in anger. This had gone too far.

"We're getting rid of the arsenal. From now on, we'll have to find other ways to protect ourselves."

39

Elder Matthew existed no more. He was given full clearance by Drysdale, the only person who knew the secret of Typha's parentage, and his new role was embraced by the resistance. Giving up his Biblically inspired name, he adopted the name by which Jasmine always preferred to call him: Condor. It was both a code name and a loving nickname, but now it was the name by which he would be known to everyone.

He threw himself into the resistance as if determined to make up for the lost years when he served, albeit halfheartedly, on the council that was responsible for so much catastrophe. He began to read voraciously, going through the books in the collection at a speed that astounded even Typha, herself a rapid reader. He began to serve on the book preservation project, reading books aloud to Annapolis, who painstakingly entered every precious word into their preservation database.

Typha continued her dual life, half above ground as she struggled to maintain the plant cultures against a growing threat from rapidly mutating bacteria, and half below ground, where she, Aspen, and Drysdale continued the work her great-grandmother started so many years ago.

Heathrow continued to work alongside her, still David by day but sloughing off his obedient identity regularly to participate in the life of a rebel. Aspen kept a close eye on him. He was confident of Heathrow's commitment to the resistance, but he wanted to make sure he didn't make any inroads with Typha, who remained blissfully oblivious of the rivalry brewing between the two young men who loved her deeply.

Typha discovered a couple of antidotes to the bacteria and made progress against the disease; unfortunately, as bacteria will, they mutated rapidly and several resistant strains had already developed. As a result, the lab was in a constant race against time, trying to develop new antibiotics faster than the bacteria could evolve. In order to keep up with everything they petitioned the elders for another employee, and the elders obliged by sending them Seth, a young man with a big ego and a chip on his shoulder, who chafed at spending his days moving cultures around and taking orders from a woman.

Typha suggested to Heathrow that maybe he should function as Seth's supervisor but he rejected her suggestion with a grin. He felt their young employee needed to adjust his mind to a few realities of life and he refused to give any relief to the pouting adolescent. In fact, every time Typha issued instructions to Seth she suspected Heathrow was behind her, grinning in jubilation at the younger man's dismay.

Every day brought a new challenge, which wasn't totally unpleasant in such a truncated world. For the first time Typha felt like a real scientist, setting up experiments, bustling around with her specimens and her cultures, and keeping neat, well organized logs of her data. She spent many hours hunched over her microscopes and her cultures, leaving most of the routine work of keeping the cultures alive to Heathrow, who was now able to operate the lab without supervision or guidance. Even with Seth's less than able assistance, things ran smoothly.

Everything changed one Saturday afternoon. Typha was in the experimental laboratory, checking cultures she had inoculated with bacteria and an antidote. Seth was sullenly wiping off chrome counters in the culture maintenance room. Heathrow was adjusting oxygen vents to make sure the right amount of gas was released at the right time when the door flew open and several members of the security force raced in.

Looking from Seth to Heathrow, they demanded "Which one of you is David?" Seth pointed an accusing finger at Heathrow and slunk behind one of the large incubators, out of sight of the guards. "We've come to collect you for your appointment with the elders", they announced, grabbing him by the collar of his jacket and thrusting him out the door. Without a further word, they moved with brisk efficiency in the direction of the council chambers.

Typha heard the commotion and stepped out to see what was going on. The lab looked empty; she spied Seth cowering behind the incubator and beckoned him to come out. He shook his head. She went behind the incubator and pulled him out into the center of the large room.

"What happened?" she asked. "Where's H...David?"

Seth shook his head, unable to force any words around the lump in his throat, and pointed to the door.

"Did he leave?"

Seth shook his head.

"Was he taken out by the guards?" she demanded, with increasing fear in her voice.

Seth nodded.

Typha raced into the hallway and caught a glimpse of the guards as they rounded the corner, shoving someone…probably Heathrow…in front of them. She started after them but stopped. She knew if they were taking him to the elders, or to the interrogators, there was nothing she could do on her own. She needed help.

Typha finished adjusting the oxygen vents and set them so they would run automatically, perhaps as long as 24 hours. She told Seth he could go home as soon as he finished cleaning up; she was going to be gone for a few minutes. Pulling off her lab coat, she raced toward the nearest rabbit hole as quickly as she could make her way through the crowded streets. Throwing caution to the winds, she flung herself down the hole, forgetting to check to see if she was being followed.

Aspen and Annapolis were in the library, working on the book preservation project, when Typha burst in.

"Where's Drysdale?" she asked breathlessly.

Aspen looked up, happy to see her so unexpectedly, but the look on her face silenced any greeting.

"He's in the main meeting room, on a conference call with Dublin", Annapolis informed her. "Why? What's wrong?"

"It's Heathrow." Typha spoke rapidly, her words tumbling over each other in her anxiety. "He's been taken away by the guards, presumably to meet with the council of elders. I suspect he's going to be taken to the Interrogators".

Aspen frowned. This was serious indeed. Although there was no reason to suspect Heathrow would sell them out deliberately, he hadn't been with the resistance very long and hadn't completed his torture training, which was designed to help resist the efforts of the Interrogators to get information. They couldn't be certain if he would have the fortitude to swallow the poison in the vial he was issued. They'd have to take immediate measures to prevent catastrophe.

"We should never have let him go back up into the world until he'd finished his torture training", Aspen muttered.

He was worried Drysdale may have trusted too much when he suggested Heathrow was secure for now.

"Now we're going to have to make sure he's able to resist. I don't know how we're going to do that. We have no way of going inside the Interrogation labyrinth."

"What about Condor?" Annapolis suggested. "He's been a member of the council of elders. Perhaps he can get inside."

"Not a chance", Drysdale said quietly from behind Annapolis, making the younger man jump. "From the moment he disappeared he was bound to be fingered as a traitor and any attempt to get into the Interrogation chambers is only going to confirm that."

Drysdale dropped onto the sofa and closed his eyes, deep in thought. He muttered to himself, "What would Jasmine do?" as he contemplated the serious situation they were faced with.

"She would sacrifice herself to save the resistance", Typha said. "That's why I'm going to go in. Someone needs to tend to the situation, and that means making sure Heathrow is strong enough to withstand the pressure or committed enough to swallow the poison. I'm the person he most trusts. I'll go."

"No!" shouted all three men at once. Drysdale continued, "You need to remain in the lab, tending the cultures. Too much depends on it for you to be absent or risk being captured again. There's no one else trained besides you. I think that's probably why they grabbed Heathrow instead of you. They realized after the last time that they couldn't play such risky games again, but they wanted to send us a message, let us know you still aren't safe. I'll go."

"I'm going with you", Aspen announced.

Drysdale shook his head but the younger man remained firm in his resolve. There was no way he was going to let Drysdale face this alone. Silently, the two men packed up a kit of things they would need. This wouldn't be the first time the resistance ventured down into the bowels of the Interrogation Chambers, so they understood what they were facing. The risk was enormous but the risk of not going was even greater.

Aspen said a warm good-bye to Typha, gathering her into his arms and squeezing her so tight for so long she nearly lost her breath. She understood. This might be the last time they saw each other. The thought was too much to bear and she turned her head away, unable to watch as the two men set out down the dark hallways toward the elevator which would take them to the top.

Typha followed, leaving just enough time to gain a small measure of safety. Soon she was back in the lab, silently going through the necessary motions to make sure the plants were tended to and the oxygen properly vented. Seth was nowhere to be seen. He followed her instructions and went home, but without finishing the cleaning up.

Typha remained in a state of nervous agitation for two days, during which time neither she nor anyone else heard a word from Aspen or Drysdale. The two men seemed to have disappeared off the face of the earth.

Word came through the grapevine that Heathrow had indeed been handed over to the Interrogators. He'd been offered a deal by the council, or so it was reported. If he turned over information on the whereabouts of Elder Matthew, he could go free and not have to submit to Interrogation. Although Typha had doubts about the integrity of the elders and the likelihood of their keeping their promise, it still reflected well on Heathrow that he hadn't sold out Condor or anyone else in the resistance. She hoped, against all the odds, that Aspen would be able to rescue him. It didn't seem likely; in fact, the most likely scenario was Aspen and Drysdale being captured and subjected to interrogation. Typha's dreams were filled with terrors and she began to stay awake around the clock, unable to defeat the demons which mocked her as she slept.

Monday evening, Typha rested on the sofa in the library. She closed her eyes but the torment which raged in her brain wouldn't allow her to sit calm. Now she was wide-eyed and alert and the weight of her sorrow and exhaustion prevented her from resting comfortably. She paced, sat down, jumped up and paced again, pulled books out of the shelves and thumbed through them, her tired eyes unable to comprehend the words on the page.

The door behind her burst open and before she knew what was happening she was swept up in a giant, familiar embrace. As she nestled her face into Aspen's neck, overcome by the familiar smell of him, she heard Drysdale outside the door, giving instructions to not be disturbed for a few minutes.

Typha nestled on the sofa between Aspen and Drysdale, her eyes glazed with sorrow. They managed to breach the security of the labyrinth and found the cell where Heathrow was held. He'd already begun his interrogation and was barely conscious, but was able to

165

recognize the men. They didn't go into details but Typha didn't need or want them; she knew all too well what he had been subjected to, and she could imagine the bruises and the blood.

He was still lucid enough to tell them he hadn't revealed any secrets yet, but he wasn't sure he could hold on much longer. Aspen gave him a vial of painkillers, which he swallowed eagerly. This gave him relief enough to endure a short conversation with the two men he only recently learned to call friend. Without any further ceremony, he pulled out the vial of poison and broke it on the wall of his cell. Within moments, Heathrow died.

Typha listened to the men tell her the tale of their entry and their escape but without actually hearing. She was overcome with grief but she wasn't able to cry. Strange...she hadn't cried when her mother died, either. That time, she just collapsed. This time, she sat in stunned silence. She'd seen a great deal of death in her short life, so much that few deaths could elicit more than a superficial grieving anymore, but the death of Heathrow rendered her immobile with grief.

She was surprised by the intensity of her feelings. She tried to tell herself to stiffen up; after all, she'd expected his death ever since he was seized by the elders. Over the past two days, she'd been expecting even worse. She expected Aspen and Drysdale wouldn't make it out alive either, and here they were, not only alive but unharmed. She still couldn't shake off the overwhelming grief washing over her.

Condor joined them and they sat in silence for a few minutes after the tale was complete. No one was able to say anything; Heathrow hadn't been with the resistance very long but he'd been a valued member and a valued friend. Typha realized if it weren't for him, she wouldn't be here today. His visits to her helped keep her going through the worst of the Interrogation, and his ability to speak the language of the elders set in motion the events which led to her eventual release.

"He sent you a message."

There was a strange sound in Aspen's voice and a look on his face Typha had never seen before. She nestled closer, feeling a coldness down her spine. Drysdale handed her a crumpled paper. She smoothed it out, reading the last words Heathrow had spoken, words set down faithfully in Aspen's neat handwriting.

166

"My dearest Typha. I've wanted to tell you something for a long time, in fact since the day I met you. I love you. I've loved you from the very first – the sound of your voice, the sparkle in your eyes, the way the light flashes when it catches the highlights in your hair. I've never known a woman like you. I allowed myself to dream that someday you and I might be married; we might have children, little girls who would have sparkling green eyes and flashing red hair. Girls who would be scientists like their mother. I couldn't bear to see you dying in the hands of the Interrogators; I saw you dying before my eyes. I wanted to take you in my arms, hold you, tell you how much I loved you, but I didn't dare. I was scared. Can you ever forgive me for my cowardice? I know now it was never meant to be. I knew it from the moment I first saw you with Aspen. My heart broke that night, but I knew he was better for you than I could ever be. He is a fighter; I'm just King David, a mythical character who could never possibly live up to legend. I wish I could say good-bye to you in person, but I'm glad Drysdale wouldn't let you come. You'd have never gotten out of here again. Good-bye, Typha. Think of me fondly now and then. Love forever, Heathrow".

Typha finished reading, barely aware the words on the paper were blurred from her tears. All those times she brushed against him and he shuddered; he wasn't disgusted. The tears began to flow and she sobbed uncontrollably against Aspen's chest. He grieved with her, holding her as he held her the horrible night her mother died. He vowed, if it was in his power, she would never have to cry again.

That night, throughout the resistance, candles were lit and a silent vigil was held. The members of the Ames group were the only ones who had personally met Heathrow but his fame had already spread throughout the international network. Not a single city missed the memorial. The candles burned brightly all night underground around the world; just before dawn, they were snuffed and the entire resistance was plunged into total darkness. They remained in darkness for 28 minutes, one minute for every year of Heathrow's life. Their fallen dead honored, they moved on. There was no time to lose in mourning.

40

Anna and Jasmine stood side by side on the podium, an old woman and her beautiful young granddaughter. They had been invited by a sorority at the University of Arkansas to make a presentation about pre-transformation history. For most of these girls, about Jasmine's age, this was ancient history and the things Anna talked about were difficult for them to comprehend.

There were no longer any recognized sororities on this campus, or on any other campus throughout the nation. This was an underground group, a group of women who studied and learned in secret classrooms, taught by women of Anna's generation who refused to recognize the authority of the new order to keep them from using their brains and talents.

These were bright, eager young women, ready to join the resistance, and sure success was only a few years away. Anna wished she could be as confident. After two decades, it was no longer possible to perceive change as just around the corner. Besides, most of the leaders of the resistance were getting old and tired. Anna looked out over the sea of young faces in front of her and hope sprang to life again. These women, she thought, these women will keep on with the work when the rest of us aren't able to maintain it anymore.

Behind the two women, a screen bore scenes of the pre-transformation world. The audience leaned forward eagerly, watching with awe and delight as women walked unhampered around college campuses, tramped in wetlands with hip waders covering their shapely legs, or bent over microscopes. This was the world they could only dream of and it was encouraging to realize it once really existed. The pictures Anna showed them depicted a world where the sun shone brightly and people smiled. It bore little resemblance to the dark, fearful world their history books told them existed before the transformation.

Two young men passed through the aisles, passing out flyers and informational brochures. Drysdale and Romaine were among the first generation of babies born underground and were totally committed to the resistance. They were among the students Anna taught in the makeshift classrooms which were established after moving underground. They were rising to prominence in the resistance, and this was their first event. Jasmine, however, attended many, being a regular fixture on the podium since the age of five. Anna glanced at her and a fond smile crossed her face. She wouldn't have to worry about much with Jasmine standing ready to take over, especially with others like Drysdale and Romaine on board to assist.

A prolonged question and answer period followed a showing of two of the films Kathy and Jason prepared for instructional and recruitment purposes. Usually they were on hand for these events but Jason was recovering from a bad case of pneumonia and Kathy stayed behind to look after him. Anna worried about working without her reliable back ups, but the two young men who accompanied her in their place proved more than equal to the job.

When the presentation was over, the girls retired to a large, barren room which served as a kitchen. They had prepared refreshments for the entire group and Anna was touched. Already resources were becoming scarce, with populations around the world exploding and putting pressure on food production. Many fields were paved over to make room for housing, and for large churches which appeared like mushrooms almost overnight. The council of elders appeared unconcerned about the food shortage, constantly exhorting citizens to pray, and assuring them God would take care of everything they might need. Most of the citizens were so numbed by years of faithful obedience to divine commands they didn't complain. After all, if they were hungry, wasn't it God's will?

Small groups of young women clustered around Anna, Jasmine, and the two young men. Anna answered all their questions as completely as possible but with an emptiness that wouldn't quite be banished. It didn't feel right still, even after a year, attending events like this without Simon. His death left a large hole in the home they built underground and nothing would ever be able to fill that hole. Anna was glad he died quietly, in his sleep, his heart simply ceasing to beat. He hadn't had a prolonged illness and he managed to be active to the end. It was the way Anna always hoped they'd both go. Somehow it never occurred to her one of them would go before the other. They'd done everything together for so long, she just assumed they would manage to die together, as well.

Her reverie was broken when she spotted Jasmine waving to her. Breaking away from the group surrounding her, she headed to the small cluster of girls around Jasmine. Some question arose that Jasmine was unable to answer and she needed Anna's help.

Focusing her mind on the task at hand and resolutely banishing Simon's memory to the background, Anna moved around the room, making sure she greeted each and every young woman personally before the reception was over. She was encouraged by the sheer numbers of young women in the room…this group managed to gather over a hundred.

The resistance would live on, Anna thought as she shook the last hand, hugged the last young rebel, and passed into the cloak of night which prevented the guards from following her to the closest rabbit hole. As Anna plunged into the earth, holding Jasmine by one hand and Drysdale by the other, she reflected on the future. Yes, she thought again, the resistance will live on.

41

Things were bad in the streets; the homeless were restless and the rest of the population was hungry. The manna was rationed more tightly because the unrest in Africa shut down many of the supply routes. The council took the precaution of doubling the guards on the street and the curfews were earlier than ever. Television time was increased and the citizens were now expected to remain in front of the set for additional shows extolling the virtues of family, country, church, and conformity.

Every day Typha went to work through crowds of homeless with dead eyes and she felt the fear and the anger in the air around her. Children with dull, matted hair clung to their mother's skirts as they tried to find a trace of left over manna clinging to the bowls set out by the curb waiting for the day's allotment. Young men became bolder about stealing allotments in broad day light and the guards were not able to keep up with the increasing crime.

In the lab, Typha was sheltered from sounds of the fighting in the street, but as she picked her way home at night she encountered pockets of violence. The resistance was on the move and was openly challenging the authority of the elders. Thanks to their foresight, they had adequate supplies of the unpleasant but necessary manna and they began to utilize some of the surplus to feed the homeless and the hungry. People began looking to the resistance for leadership and solutions. The resistance opened up impromptu rescue shelters in the streets and welcomed all who wanted something to eat. The council was having trouble ignoring the consequences of their actions and Typha knew things were about to come to a head.

It was a Sunday afternoon when the resistance struck. Just as church let out, all over the country the resistance forces waited. As people filed out of the church doors, resistance fighters streamed in and took over the last remaining areas which weren't swarming with people.

The occupation proved easy; most of the preachers were soft and complacent, not used to being challenged, and they had no counter strategy. All the church leaders were taken prisoner and the churches opened as sanctuaries for the homeless. The soft pews proved popular as people who were without a bed for years took possession.

Soon all the churches were full of people, hungry people, being fed for the first time in days. The resistance was moving and the elders were feeling pressed. They were losing where it counted; the underground opened hospitals, schools, nurseries, and soup kitchens. Instead of fear, people received kindness and much needed sustenance. The church bells rang the beginning of a new day, a day in which the elders would have no power and people would govern themselves. It was a heady time for those who lived their life underground for so long, waiting and watching for the slightest chink in the armor of the elders.

Just as suddenly as it began, it was over. The elders had issued commands for days, commands which were ignored by the resistance and the citizens who had come to depend on them. After two weeks of stand-off, the elders opened the doors of the central compounds in cities all over the world and slaves they had nurtured and trained came pouring out, armed to the teeth with guns, knives, and other weaponry most of the citizens didn't possess. Although the resistance was trained in hand-to-hand combat, they found themselves outnumbered as terrified citizens, fearful the battle could only go to the elders, fearful of men who got their commands directly from God, and used to obedience to a centralized authority, turned back to the elders and began to surround resistance members, taking them prisoner or clubbing them to death with any hard object they could find. The Council cheered them on, setting up regular broadcasts explaining how the current famine was the result of God's unhappiness because the resistance had been allowed to flourish for so long.

The resistance moved back underground, decimated and demoralized. Their small numbers were no match for the forces of habit and obedience. In spite of all the hunger and the despair which seized hold of the lives of the people, most of them chose an illusion of safety over freedom. Unable to face the unfamiliarity of making their own day-to-day decisions, they turned on the resistance as quickly as they'd turned on the elders.

As the governments in Africa got their citizens back in line, the supply lines began to open up and manna was again available. The people moved back into the familiar conformity of their lives, eating manna when they could get it, going to work, reproducing, and watching television.

The resistance was able to bring a few of their fallen comrades underground for burial, but most of them were left behind to be cremated in the furnaces of the elders. The tenor of life underground began to stabilize again, returning to the normal pattern and rhythm of life before the uprising. Once again the resistance was hiding, waiting for any opportunity to subvert the dominant order. Security above was doubled, even tripled in places, and the wait became even more dangerous than before.

42

Anna faced the man with the bulldozer. All around her beloved prairie and wetland, condos and apartments rose out of the broken soil. Her little preserve was all that remained. She was determined they should never move onto this small patch of ground, not while she had breath in her body to defeat them. Behind her, Kathy, Jason, and Jasmine formed another line of defense, backing her up to the last. Drysdale and Romaine flanked her, supporting her frail frame with their sturdy, solid young bodies. The resistance solidified around protecting a tiny patch of earth from the ravages of runaway population growth and total ecological obliviousness.

Ever since the transformation, species preservation and natural habitats were deemed irrelevant. The human species was the one that mattered. If God wanted prairie dogs and polar bears to survive, why, he would take care of them and ensure their success. Since the polar bear no longer existed, obviously God had little use for their continued survival. Nearly all the large fauna, except for a handful of food animals, were rendered extinct as swollen human populations encroached on their last remaining refuges.

Trees were felled, wetlands drained and filled, and prairies paved. The sky grew darker and more toxic by the day but the council of elders didn't appear to notice the problem. Whenever a new crisis arose, they appeared, called a prayer vigil, and disappeared back into the isolation of the central council chambers. All the cities around the world were governed by a council and all the cities had their own large compound to house the rulers, who remained insulated from the general public.

The resistance periodically engaged in acts of vandalism directed at these centers of command, but in the end it was like a mosquito stinging an elephant. The thick perimeter of the large structures proved difficult, perhaps impossible, to breach, and they had to be content with minor mischief which was largely dismissed by the elders as irrelevant. From time to time they did get a rise out of the elders, usually by some wag who painted something blasphemous against the Christian God on the walls and bridges around the town. Mostly, however, they were just banging their heads in frustration against impregnable walls.

As the bulldozers rumbled forward, Anna thrust out her chin with determination. Brushing a stray lock of her silver hair back from her forehead, she raised her hand, asking for silence. She raised a megaphone to her lips and her voice, strangely strong for a frail, elderly woman, rang out with the speech she prepared years ago for this occasion. A true ecological manifesto, rejecting the concept of constant growth of human numbers, speaking out against the race to win the population sweepstakes, and sounding a clarion call for protection of the few remaining refuges for wildlife, she captivated the watching crowd for over an hour.

All the members of the Ames resistance were present, and many of the international leaders. The organization went into rapid response mode as soon as it became obvious the desires of the private ownership of this one little patch of ground were no longer going to be respected. Anna felt Simon strong and silent beside her, his love holding her up even though he was no longer present in the flesh. Jasmine took the megaphone and added a few words of her own, and the formal part of the rally was finished. The resistance members surged forward, forming a ring around Anna in solidarity against the large machinery they faced off against.

The dozer operators surveyed the scene in front of them. Nothing in their training prepared them for this. Young men, still in their childhood when the transformation occurred, they knew nothing of the many rebellions throughout the world's history and didn't expect anyone to turn out to protect a useless swamp and an empty prairie.

The foreman dialed his phone furiously, attempting to get instructions from the home office of the company. Until that, they just sat on their machines, waiting them out. The woman leading them was so old and so frail, she couldn't manage to hold on for long. They were sure it would be over in minutes.

All sorts of technical problems plagued the project and today the cell phones weren't working correctly. It seemed hardly anything worked correctly anymore. Whenever anything broke, they were told to pray and someone would eventually show up to fix it. Some things did get fixed. Many things didn't. There simply weren't enough technicians to go around, and God didn't seem too eager to provide more. So they waited. When the call came telling them what to do, then they could move. When the old lady got tired and went home, they could move.

The standoff continued for hours. The morning became afternoon and the afternoon faded into evening. The bulldozer operators shifted uncomfortably in their seats, unwilling to leave their posts even to get a drink of water or use the bathroom. The resistance brought food and water and sat cross-legged on the banks of the wetland, enjoying a tasty looking picnic. Where did they manage to get the food? the workmen wondered. Food was so scarce and so expensive these days, they must have a special source. They began to long for a sandwich or even just a small piece of dry bread.

Anna took pity on the workmen. After all, they were only doing their job. Wrapping up several sandwiches, she sent Jasmine and Drysdale over to offer food to the men waiting silently on their giant machines. The men accepted the sandwiches gratefully but almost spoiled the deal by leering at Jasmine. Drysdale was fuming when he returned to the picnic.

"Did you see them?" he shouted. "They looked at Jasmine as though she was some sort of pretty toy for them to play with. You fed the enemy! What's up?"

Anna patiently took him to task, reminding him gently that keeping your ethical principles intact was even more important now as the world shifted seismically around them. Drysdale always did have a temper but Anna worked with him patiently for the past several years, helping him learn to control himself and approach problems rationally and calmly. He was learning well and had the makings of a good leader, but he was very protective of Jasmine, and the slightest insult to her or any of the other women of the resistance really got his dander up. Now that he was in his adolescence, he'd gotten even more protective.

Shortly before sunset the foreman's phone rang. The phone service had been restored and he was back in contact with the home office. He spoke with the office for several minutes, explaining the situation, then listening obediently. He became increasingly more agitated. It was obvious he didn't like what he heard but he knew he was obliged to obey orders. He was receiving orders directly from the council of elders, and they were not to be questioned.

The call completed, the foreman spoke quietly with the machine operators. Anna and Jason tried to get a feel for what they were saying, but they were too far away to hear anything. The men on the dozers frowned, shaking their head and protesting. What were the orders they received?

The foreman was puzzled. All his life, he'd been taught that above all else, you must respect and protect human life. You must never, ever, consider doing anything which would threaten the life of a human being, no matter how small and fragile, even if the human wasn't yet born. Now he was being told he was to order his bulldozers to drive right through the crowd, to plow them down if need be, and do the job he'd been hired to do.

He couldn't believe his ears. There was a little old lady in charge and she certainly couldn't withstand an onslaught like that. He always respected his elders and was unwilling to do what he'd been told. He wasn't given a choice in the matter, but was told it was God's will. If God wanted the people in the crowd to survive, he would protect them. As he passed these peculiar orders on to his men, he met with a great deal of resistance.

These were good men, decent men, and they were just doing a job. They didn't want to run over anyone, particularly not those nice, decent people who were willing to share a meal with people they regarded as the enemy. The orders were final. There was no arguing allowed. In disgust, half of the workers deserted their posts, leaving their bulldozers behind forever and taking a stand with the people guarding the wetland. They were now and forevermore in resistance.

As the ranks of the resistance swelled with new members, Anna faced her wetland. She knew what the orders were; she'd known from the beginning what the orders would likely be. The elders demonstrated years ago they had little patience with those who opposed their plans. Many of the resistance had been seized and never seen again. The president had been assassinated.

At first the bodies were dumped where they would be easily found and the resistance was given the opportunity to bury their dead. Lately, though, the disappearances were complete. They never saw their fallen friends again. Many of them were taken off for "Interrogation", a process so brutal and so painful the resistance began providing torture training to help members withstand the pain enough not to provide valuable information to the elders. They began carrying small vials of fast-acting poison in case the pain got too severe. Loyal members preferred to sacrifice themselves rather than betray the resistance.

Anna knew the wetland was gone. These were men with no limits to their power and no limits to their determination. She said good-bye for the last time to her beloved wetland, to the snakes she and Jasmine painstakingly catalogued, to the plants she carefully introduced in her restoration attempts. The cattails waved in the breeze and she allowed herself to imagine that they were acknowledging her thoughts and telling her not to blame herself.

Her good-byes said, Anna turned her back to the wetland and faced the bulldozers defiantly. The members of the resistance crowded around her in solidarity but she waved them away.

"Don't stand here", she said. "The bulldozers are coming."

"Mom!" Jason yelled. "You've got to move away. You can't stand there!"

"I must, sweetie. Don't mourn for me. I've had a good long life. This is what I have to do now."

Anna blew him and his family a kiss, the final kiss. "You must continue the fight. You must keep the resistance strong. They'll need you. They'll need Jasmine."

"Mom!" Kathy grabbed Jason as his voice rang across the prairie. She tore him away from his mother, holding him tight as her eyes filled with tears and she whispered a silent good-bye to the bravest woman she'd ever known, a woman she loved as a mother. She held Jasmine tight to her other side, burying the young woman's face in her neck, protecting her from the sight of her grandmother being crushed to death by a brutal enemy. Jasmine held tight to her mother but resisted Kathy's efforts to protect her; she held her gaze steady with Anna's, refusing to turn away even as her eyes burned with tears.

The setting sun shimmered through the haze of the dirty sky as the bulldozers pressed forward. One lone woman remained, defiantly facing them down. The rest of the members of the resistance scattered, standing to one side, unwilling to let her stand there alone but understanding why she couldn't step aside. She was going to die, it was obvious, but they intended her death to stand for something. If they died with her, no one would remain to carry on the work. They watched in despair and anger as the bulldozers rumbled on, three of them bearing down on a little old woman as the setting sun formed a golden halo over her silver head.

Two hours later, in the moonlight, Jason spread the last shovelful of dirt over the makeshift grave which was the final resting place of his beloved mother. Jasmine and Kathy stood nearby, their arms locked together, their heads bowed in shocked sorrow as they sang softly, an old tune Anna used to love, *The Long and Winding Road*. Scooping up a few bedraggled cattails from the side of the gaping hole the bulldozers dug in the wetland, he dropped them on her grave.

The cattails were already wilting, dying in the heat of the summer night. Without a word, Jason and the two women joined the rest of the resistance. They headed through the night without speaking, down into the bowels of the underground hideout. That night, candles would be lit all over the world. Just before dawn, they would be snuffed out simultaneously as the entire resistance plunged into darkness, a darkness which would last for 78 minutes. The cattails would remain as the only testament to the strength and courage of a woman who wouldn't be sent back to the kitchen. Soon they too would wilt and die, covered by layers of concrete to make room for one more days' worth of new babies.

43

Typha listened in horror as Condor described the inner workings of the council of elders. She was brought up by her mother to have great disrespect for this body of men, untrained in anything but church history and dogma, literate only to the point of being able to read the biblical passages they preferred, and oblivious to the suffering and loss going on around them. She had worked for them for a decade, seeing the calm quiet of their compound in contrast to the teeming mass of humanity living without homes outside. She didn't imagine anything could shock her about how the elders worked but she hadn't understood the scope and magnitude of their ignorance.

Insulated from the outside world, the council lost any idea of what happened outside the command center. They knew nothing of the poverty and hunger that was the normal state of the people they commanded. They were oblivious to the lack of adequate clean water and the masses of homeless filling the streets. Staying to themselves inside the compound, they were able to ignore the realities their policies created and convince themselves the world outside was a better, healthier, and happier place than it was before the transformation.

Condor admitted, shamefacedly, that he once believed the same things. It was only after meeting Jasmine and learning from her that he realized nothing was the way the elders believed in their happy fantasies. Now he was telling all their secrets, and the resistance listened with growing disgust to the tales of depravity that punctuated the story of the elders.

Inside the compound, the elders indulged shamelessly in all the pleasures they denied the citizens outside. There was plenty to eat and all the water you needed, protected in reservoirs behind high walls, patrolled by security in case someone from outside should discover its whereabouts. They had soft beds in large rooms with plenty of space. All their needs were met by a large staff of slaves bred specially to serve their needs. The slaves were referred to as "servants" by the elders, Condor said, but the proper word for them would be slaves.

Although they all married young, proper women who were considered suitable wives for the ruling class and fathered many children, they had no hesitation to fulfill their crassest sexual fantasies. Sex proved easy, as the slaves stood ready at any time to bring women from the outside into the compound and the women from outside were too cowed and subservient to say no. An elder gave instructions to the slave about the type of woman he wanted that night – age, hair color, figure, and anything else that mattered – and the slave would exit the compound, search until he found a woman who met all the requirements, and bring her back inside. Once finished with her, the woman would be returned to her husband or father with instructions that she must never reveal the liaison to anyone. It was God's command. The women obeyed; if they didn't, they were taken to the Interrogators. Typha shuddered.

Condor outlined the plans of the elders for the future, and the plans were grim. Typha had always assumed it was more of the same and the resistance would keep on fighting until eventually they would win and restore some level of sanity to the world. Listening to Condor, she realized the resistance would never win.

The Ames elders managed to consolidate all power and now the entire world was run from this command center. The other centers in other cities, in other countries, were just branch offices which existed more for show than for function. Typha was horrified to realize she was the reason they were able to do that. Because of her skill and dedication in the laboratory, Ames was able to maintain the tissue cultures while other labs all over the world failed, unable to figure out how to keep the plants alive. The reason this lab was able to maintain was the relationship her mother had with an elder...because he was aware of the dire situation they were in, he was able to persuade them to utilize an actual, trained scientist to run the lab. It hadn't been easy, since the scientist he had in mind was a woman, but he prevailed.

Most of the other labs around the world, after being set up by properly trained scientists, were turned over to young men hand-picked by the elders, who believed anyone would be able to maintain the labs after only a week of training; Typha thought of the parade of incompetent, arrogant assistants she'd been assigned. For the first time, she realized her lab was the only one still operational.

Typha realized nothing the resistance was going to be able to do would save the world from the folly of the elders. Even if they were able to prevail, there wasn't much left to save. Most of the species were extinct. Those which remained were the ones cultured in her lab. There was very little raw material for evolution to work with, but it had managed to build quite a world once from a very humble beginning. If they did fail, perhaps the world would someday begin again, with life restored through the natural processes which created it in the first place. Typha fell asleep puzzled by her thoughts. Her dreams were peculiar, like none she'd ever had, but she woke the next morning knowing what she needed to do.

After breakfast, Typha held a consultation with Aspen, Drysdale, Condor, and Annapolis. She outlined her plan, speaking in hushed tones as though afraid someone would overhear. At first they resisted, but they quickly realized the only hope of success lay down the path she described. They voted and agreed unanimously to leave the entire situation in Typha's hands. It wasn't the outcome they awaited for so many years, but it was the only outcome which made sense. A quick consultation brought confirmation from the international community. The resistance was behind her all the way.

The day was just beginning when Typha made her way above ground the next morning. The dome lights were not yet fully on and the dimness of the light suited her mood. She was scared. She walked slowly and thoughtfully toward the lab, picking her way through mobs of people lying on the street, just beginning to stir with the coming of the light. It was Friday and the street cleaners were out today, cleaning the dead and dying off the sidewalk and carting them to the crematorium to be disposed of in time for Sunday services. The city needed to be clean for the Sabbath.

By the time she reached the central compound the light was fully on, and the bright glare of relentless light which changed little throughout the day heralded the beginning of the work day. Men bustled around, heading off toward whatever their day held, while the women stayed in the apartments getting the children ready for school and waiting behind until the men cleared out of the streets. Typha never understood why this ritual was maintained; with all the homeless, there was never a time when the streets were clear of men. After her conversations with Condor, she realized it really was just a ritual and the ritual was simply a means of control over the populace, particularly over the women, who had formed such a tight knot of resistance in the early years following the transformation. With a heavy heart, Typha turned the key in the door of the lab.

After Seth left for the evening, Typha stayed on. She moved from incubator to incubator, adjusting knobs, testing dials, and moving things into their proper place. She checked her beloved plants and

182

noticed many more of them were infected. Tonight she didn't bother to isolate them. There really wasn't any point in it.

Just as the dome began to darken, Typha made one last round of the incubators. These plants, these small, visually insignificant tissue cultures, were the only things which stood between the human population and death. The oxygen she so faithfully vented each day was necessary to maintain the species. Now she knew that was truer than she had realized. This one lab, this shining bright clean lab she called her own, was the only remaining source of oxygen.

Typha hesitated. The step she was about to take was enormous. She hoped she had the strength. For so many years she dedicated her life to preventing anything going wrong with the vents; now she was about to turn them off for good. It didn't feel right and she paused. No, this wasn't something she could do; it wasn't something she should do. What right did she have to make such a final decision for so many people?

She sat gasping for breath, unable to make the final changes. Life…she was talking about taking not just one life, but billions of lives, hundreds of billions of faceless individuals, living their lives quietly, not even knowing what went on behind the huge gray walls which protected the compound from intrusion. She sat for several minutes, overwhelmed by the enormity of the decision she'd made and tormented by doubts. She had little doubt life would survive; the plants would continue to grow a little longer but without water, they were doomed, too. Unseen, though, there were countless tiny organisms, microbes too small to be seen, and they would live on. An immense, beautiful, diverse world had risen from the simple bacteria once; no doubt it would do so again. But…

Typha shook herself. She needed to take this action. There was no other way; the plans of the elders must never come to fruition and there was no other way to defeat them. Life would rise again, perhaps even intelligent life, and next time, perhaps they would be able to learn from the mistakes of their ancient ancestors.

Steeling herself, she went from incubator to incubator, carefully changing all the dials to close the vents. She checked to make sure no dials remained in the open position before she closed the door to the lab. When the elders realized what happened, it would be too late. Seth was never interested in learning how to maintain the cultures and he wouldn't know how to tell whether the vents were open or closed.

183

He wouldn't know how to fix them, even if he did, because Typha took great care to alter the settings so he wouldn't be able to figure out the new configuration.

Back in the underground hideout, Typha paused before the bookshelves, running her hands over the spines. These books held the entire known history of the human race; the preservation project had saved many of them. If intelligent life should ever again evolve, perhaps the new species would learn to decipher the old texts and learn about an ancient culture, a culture which existed long ago, a culture which destroyed itself by remaining ignorant of consequences. Perhaps, someday, this new culture would find the clues in these books to help prevent them from making such a disastrous mistake.

Typha lay beside Aspen. He reached for her and held her tightly in his arms. They made love for the last time, lingering over every warm caress. Just before dawn, underneath the surface of the earth, hidden from the eyes of the masses of humanity swarming above, poison capsules in hand, the members of the resistance all simultaneously snuffed their candles, plunging the entire underground world into permanent darkness.